DO N
B
BEGINNING TO END!

You just checked into the Dead Hotel.

The question is, will you check out?

That all depends on whether you can make it through the night! Because this is no ordinary hotel. It's full of ghosts who want you to be their permanent guest. And if you can't find a way to stay awake and then escape, you'll be stuck here . . . forever.

This scary adventure is all about you. You decide what will happen — and how terrifying the scares will be!

Start on PAGE 1. Then follow the instructions at the bottom of each page. You make the choices. If you choose well, you'll make it out of this haunted hotel. But if you make the wrong choice . . . BEWARE!

SO TAKE A DEEP BREATH. CROSS YOUR FINGERS. AND TURN TO PAGE 1 TO *GIVE YOURSELF GOOSEBUMPS!*

READER BEWARE —
YOU CHOOSE THE SCARE!

Look for more
GIVE YOURSELF GOOSEBUMPS adventures
from R.L. STINE:

R.L. STINE

GIVE YOURSELF

Goosebumps®

CHECKOUT TIME AT THE DEAD-END HOTEL

AN
APPLE
PAPERBACK

SCHOLASTIC INC.
New York Toronto London Auckland Sydney

A PARACHUTE PRESS BOOK

ISBN 0-590-39998-5

12 11 10 9 8 7 6 5 4 3 2 1   8 9/9 0 1 2 3/0

Printed in the U.S.A.   40

First Scholastic printing, April 1998

"Why are we slowing down *here*?" B. J. Matson moans from the front seat of the car. "It's so dark."

You open your eyes and yawn. You must have dozed off. Sleepily, you gaze out the car window. It's a misty, starless night. You're on a two-lane road in the middle of nowhere.

"Where are we?" you ask B. J.'s mom.

"I'm not sure," Mrs. Matson answers. "The car sounded funny, so I pulled off the highway. We need to have a mechanic look at the engine."

You nudge Moira O'Neil. She's sleeping beside you in the backseat. Then you reach across her and poke Jamie Kaplan in the leg. You, Jamie, Moira, and B. J. are on a class trip to Washington, D.C. You're supposed to stay in a motel when you get there.

But B. J.'s mother is a slow driver. The other parents' cars vanished down the highway a long time ago.

Mrs. Matson pulls off the deserted road. You peer out the window. There's nothing in sight except a sign for a hotel.

"Wake up," you whisper nervously to Moira and Jamie. "We're stopping — at a place called the Dead Hotel!"

Go on to PAGE 2.

Moira's eyes snap open. She leans across you and stares out. You peer into the darkness as Mrs. Matson pulls up the driveway.

You spot a huge old hotel with dark stone columns flanking the entrance. The building is set back from the road, among some pine trees. There are strange carvings over the front door. Gargoyles gaze down at you.

"The sign doesn't say Dead Hotel," Moira argues. "It says Hotel Morte."

"Yeah," you agree. "But do you know what 'morte' means? It means death — in about sixteen languages! You know — like *mort*ician. And *mort*al. And —"

"That's enough." Mrs. Matson sighs. "The only thing that's dead is my car. Hop out — we're spending the night here."

You, Moira, B. J., and Jamie all grab your duffel bags from the trunk. Then you follow Mrs. Matson into the creepy hotel.

The instant you step into the lobby you feel a strange chill. As if an icy hand has just rubbed across your shoulders.

You glance around the marble lobby. Old leather couches and armchairs dot the huge room. Dusty potted palms lurk in the corners.

But there's not a single person in sight.

"Welcome to Hotel Morte!" a voice calls out of nowhere.

Go on to PAGE 3.

You jump, startled. Where did that voice come from?

Then you spot the desk clerk. You hadn't noticed him before. He's a scrawny man with beady little eyes. Thin strands of hair are combed across his greasy bald head.

"We only have one room left," he informs you, handing over the key. You shiver when you see the room number.

Room 1313!

You haul your bags into the rickety old elevator, press the button for thirteen, and ride up.

"Hey, this isn't so bad," Jamie says as you all pile into the room. "It's got all the regular stuff. TV, telephone, room service —"

"*Don't* call room service!" Mrs. Matson snaps. "I'm going down the hall to get us some sodas from the drink machine. I'll see if there are any snacks."

As soon as she's gone, B. J. grabs the TV remote control. "Let's watch a pay-per-view movie," he suggests. "If we hurry, my mom won't be back in time to cancel it."

"Forget the movie," Jamie argues. "Let's order some food. I'm starved!"

If you want to order room service, turn to PAGE 32.

If you'd rather watch a movie, turn to PAGE 44.

"Hey! Stop! Where are we going?" you shout at the driver.

You and Jamie exchange scared glances.

"Buckle up, chums!" the bus driver replies. "We're going for a wild ride!"

Whoa! He's not kidding!

The bus barrels around a curve — and tilts onto just one set of wheels.

A moment later, the road curves the other way. The bus driver yanks the wheel. The tires squeal.

"Awesome!" Jamie shouts. "It's like having a private roller-coaster ride! Or being on a race-car track!"

"No, it's not," you scream. "He's going to get us killed!"

"Not *all* of us," the bus driver comments cheerfully.

Uh-oh. You don't like the sound of that.

"Wh-wh-what do you mean?" you stammer.

"Well," the bus driver explains, turning to grin at you, "I can't get *myself* killed — because I'm already dead!"

Try not to scream yet. Just turn to PAGE 33.

Your head snaps around.

"Huh?" you grunt, staring at the empty bus seats.

"You saved us!" the invisible voices cry.

Then, one by one, the seats begin to fill up. With ghosts!

At first they are airy, filmy. Finally they become solid.

You stare in amazement. Your mouth falls open.

Every single seat in the bus is filled with ghosts.

But not ordinary ghosts.

They're the ghosts of circus performers!

Turn to PAGE 43.

The hideous ghost unlocks the door of the pillow room, letting you and Jamie out.

"This way," he whispers, motioning for you to follow. "Come quickly — before anyone sees!"

He leads you to the Bat's Ballroom. It's a huge room with red velvet drapes at the windows. Red and gold carpeting covers the floor. Images of flapping bats are woven into it.

You hurry across the carpet, toward the far end of the room. There the old ghost pulls back a long, red velvet drape. Behind it is a solid oak panel. He knocks on the panel twice. It opens!

Jamie lets out a low whistle. "Cool!"

"Shhhhh!" the ghost warns. "If the others catch us here, we'll *all* be in trouble. They'll turn us into ghost toast!"

Hidden behind the panel is a red door. The ghost opens it. You peer into the darkness and realize it's a hallway. A very long, dark hallway.

"After you." The ghost gestures for you to go in first.

You shudder. That dark hallway gives you the creeps. Maybe you and Jamie should head back to your room.

Step into the secret hallway on PAGE 70.
Go back to your room on PAGE 134.

You spend the rest of the night searching for Moira, B. J., and B. J.'s mom — and running from the ghosts.

They seem to be everywhere now. More and more of them.

As daylight approaches, they float out of the walls. Old ghosts. Young. Moaning. Crying. Laughing.

They scare you so much, you just want to hide. But you know you have to keep searching for your friends.

At least your terror keeps you awake!

Finally you find B. J., Moira, and B. J.'s mom — in the basement. Hiding in a laundry cart. Under a pile of sheets.

Quickly you explain everything that's happened. About Drew Mortegarth, and about the new checkout time.

"We can get out," you tell them. "But we need your watch, B. J. What time is it?"

B. J. glances at his watch and gasps. "It's 10:57!" he cries. "We've only got three minutes!"

Uh-oh.

"We've got to run!" you cry, dashing for the stairs.

Hurry back to Jamie and Drew on PAGE 50.

Your heart pounds in fear. But your eyelids feel heavy. The soft music and dim lights are making you sleepy.

It doesn't help that it's almost midnight. You were tired even before you checked into this haunted hotel!

"Sleep . . . ," a soothing voice begins to croon. "Sleeeeep . . ."

"No!" you shout. "We won't!"

But Jamie's shoulders slump. He looks drowsy.

"We've got to stay awake!" you order Jamie. "Come on — jump. Sing songs. Do something — *anything*! Just stay awake!"

"Okay." Jamie nods. "But let's play a game or something. How about if we try to name the Seven Dwarfs?"

The Seven Dwarfs? That's too hard, you think. Besides, isn't that kind of like counting sheep? It might make you *more* sleepy.

Jamie's eyelids droop.

You've got to do something fast, to keep him awake.

Quick. Choose one!

If you decide to sing songs and dance, turn to PAGE 51.

If you try to name the Seven Dwarfs, turn to PAGE 18.

With a sober face, Drew tells you his whole story.

"I'm the last of the Mortegarth family," he explains. "My great-grandfather built this hotel — but it's been bad luck from the beginning. First my great-grandfather died while he was staying in Room 402. Then every single one of my relatives died there. Some by accident. Some were murdered. Their ghosts came back and took over. They started haunting the place — and turning all the employees and guests into ghosts! Now, everyone who stays here ends up dead by morning."

"But why didn't you die?" Jamie asks, his eyes wide. "I mean, you sleep here every night — right?"

Drew nods. "The ghosts can't hurt me because I'm a Mortegarth," he explains.

You gulp. "But . . . but . . . you called us!" you blurt out. "You said you had the key! To get us out!"

Drew hangs his head down, looking guilty. "I lied," he admits. "I'm trapped here too. I wanted you to come find me — so you could help *me* find a way out."

You and Jamie exchange looks. Terrified looks.

"We're sunk!" Jamie moans. "Totally sunk!"

Sink — or maybe swim — on PAGE 27.

10

You can't resist. You have to find out who spoke.
You creep toward the closet door.

You can feel Jamie holding his breath. Waiting.
Tense.

Silently, you place your hand on the doorknob.
With a quick jerk, you yank the door open wide.

"Ahhhh!" a voice shouts.

And someone leaps out at you!

Jump out of the way on PAGE 15.

Your skin crawls as you stare at the piles of skeletons.

There must be thousands of them. Stacked to the ceiling!

A single fat candle sits in a black iron holder on the wall. It lights the basement room, casting strange shadows.

You take a step forward. Then freeze.

What was that?

Footsteps?

"Who's there?" you call. Your voice trembles.

For a moment, all is silent. Then someone steps out of the shadows.

"Moira?" you gasp.

"Are they gone?" Moira's voice quavers with fear.

"Are who gone?"

"The ghosts," she replies. "Two horrible ones. They chased me down the steps and then left me here. One was an old woman — with a knife sticking out of her chest!"

Moira is about to say more. But she stops. Her eyes widen.

You both jerk your heads in the direction of the skeletons.

Something's moving!

Turn to PAGE 21.

"We're ghosts!" you cry, shivering and rubbing your arms to keep warm.

"Awesome," Jamie exclaims, his teeth chattering.

"What's so awesome about it?" you moan. "We're stuck here in this creepy hotel forever — and we'll never see any of our other friends again!"

"Who says?" Jamie replies, jumping to his ghostly feet.

Before you know it, Jamie floats away. Passing through walls. Flying upward.

You don't know how you do it, but you follow him. Just by using your mind, you are able to go anywhere you want to go.

Instantly.

When you stop floating, you find yourself back in Room 1313 — the room you started in.

"What are we doing here?" you ask Jamie.

He doesn't answer you. He just rummages through B. J.'s mom's purse until he finds a slip of paper.

"Got it!" Jamie cries, holding up the paper triumphantly.

"Got what?" you demand.

Find out on PAGE 60.

You remember all those cans of clam juice in the fridge in Room 402.

"It's the kid," you whisper so only Jamie can hear you.

You and Jamie turn and dash toward the boy.

"Come on, Drew!" Jamie shouts at him. "Let's run!"

Drew spins around. The three of you bolt out of the dining room as if twenty monsters were chasing you.

Actually, no one's chasing you. Not even the woman in the red dress. She's not fast enough in her high heels.

But you can hear her voice, laughing, as you speed away. "Ha-ha-ha!" she calls. "Fools! You'll never escape."

You follow Drew Mortegarth through the lobby and down a long hall to a broom closet. When you are all inside, he locks the door.

"What are we doing in here?" Jamie demands, out of breath. "Just give us the keys so we can get out of the hotel!"

Drew's dark eyes seem to reflect no light. "I can't give you the keys," he says softly, a sad note in his voice.

"Why not?" you demand. You swallow hard.

Did you make the wrong choice?

Learn the truth on PAGE 9.

"Check out that light," you murmur to Jamie. "I bet there's a house up there. In the woods."

Jamie nods. "Let's hike up and see."

Good idea!

There *is* a house up there.

Too bad you didn't realize that your face, shirt, and hair are all covered with doggie drool. And doggie drool has a scent to it. A strong scent!

Especially to other animals. Like wolves. They can smell your doggie-slop face a mile away!

WOOF! HOWWLLLL! WOOF-WOOF!

The wolves in the woods descend from the hills and make a quick meal out of you and Jamie.

Oh, well. Next time, try going out through a *cat* door. At least you might survive longer that way. Cats have nine lives!

THE END

You scream, leaping out of the way.

"Ah! Ha-ha-ha-ha!" Jamie sputters behind you. "It's Moira!"

"Moira?" you squeak. "What are *you* doing here?"

Moira gives you a sneaky smile. "Hiding," she explains, looking pleased with herself. "Hiding from the ghosts."

You shake your head. "Well, don't do that!" you complain. "I mean, don't jump out and scare me! This place is creepy enough."

"I know," Moira replies. "I just couldn't help it. I heard your voices, and I thought it would be fun."

You roll your eyes. "Some fun," you snap.

"Don't get nasty," Moira snaps back. "Or I won't take you to Drew Mortegarth."

Your eyes open wide. "You *found* Drew Mortegarth?"

Turn to PAGE 57.

You edge up to the huge pile of skeletons.

A skull glares at you. Or at least it seems that way. The head is facing you. At eye level.

A shudder runs down your spine. But something draws you closer. You really want to touch the bones.

"Let me try," you tell Moira. "I want to hear them too."

Whoa. Big mistake!

The minute your fingers grip the bones, the whole pile of skeletons begins to topple. They clatter and crash down on you and Moira. Knocking you over. Burying you — alive!

"Ha-ha-ha," a voice laughs. "They fell for it!"

Through the pile of bones, you watch two ghosts begin to appear. One is the ghost of an old woman — with a knife sticking out of her chest. The other is of a young boy.

"That's them!" Moira gasps. "The ghosts who chased me!"

Face the ghosts on PAGE 40.

"Forget the doggie door," Jamie says. "We can't fit through there. Let's find Mortegarth."

You eye the small opening. You decide Jamie is right.

"Okay," you reply. "But we need a plan for finding Mortegarth. I say we take the elevator to the top floor and work our way down. We should search every room."

"Great plan," Jamie comments. "Except for one thing. How are we going to get *into* all those rooms?"

"Uh, knock?" you respond, half serious, half joking.

Jamie rolls his eyes. "Yeah, right. We need keys."

"Where are we supposed to get keys?" you demand.

"The desk clerk has them," Jamie answers. "I say we sneak into the lobby, do something crazy to attract his attention, and then steal the keys."

"I don't know." You hesitate, remembering that the ghost on the TV said there weren't any *living* humans in the hotel. "What if the desk clerk is a ghost?"

"Could be," Jamie agrees. Then his eyes light up. "On the other hand, maybe the desk clerk is Drew Mortegarth! Let's go."

Jamie takes off without waiting for you.

Hurry and follow him to PAGE 24.

"Okay, we'll name the Seven Dwarfs," you tell Jamie. "You go first."

"Fine." Jamie squelches a yawn. "Dopey... Doc . . . Sneezy."

"Sleepy," you add.

"Yeah, I am," Jamie agrees. He collapses onto a pile of pillows on the floor.

"No! Not sleepy — *Sleepy*! One of the dwarfs!" you cry.

"You're right. I'm soooo sleepy . . ." Jamie shuts his eyes.

"Wake up!" you yell, shaking him.

But Jamie lies motionless.

You struggle to keep your eyes open. "Grumpy, Happy, . . ." you mumble. "How many is that?"

No answer from Jamie.

"Sleep . . ." a voice in the darkness urges. "Just close your eyes and sleeeeeep."

The voice is so soothing. So comforting. You close your eyes and sink back into the pillows.

I've never felt this tired, you think. How can that be?

Then it hits you. The room must be cursed!

"Sweet dreams," the voice murmurs, coming closer to you.

You're in big trouble unless you can stay awake on PAGE 108.

You and Jamie slowly approach the woman.

"Are you really Drew Mortegarth?" you ask.

"No — she's not!" a voice calls from behind you. "Don't believe her!"

You whirl around. You discover a kid about your age crawling out from under a dining table near the door.

The kid has reddish hair and a round face with freckles. He looks like a nice, ordinary guy. Until you glance at his eyes. They are so dark, they're almost black. They give him a creepy, serious expression.

"*I'm* Drew Mortegarth," the kid insists. "*I* called you. Don't trust her. She's a ghost!"

Jamie glances at you nervously. "Uh, which one is the real one?" he whispers under his breath.

Good question.

Do you know?

Turn to PAGE 56.

You decide to answer the phone.

"Hello?" you say.

"Listen carefully," a strange, whispery voice orders on the other end of the line. You can't tell if it's a man or a woman speaking. Or even a kid.

"I am Drew Mortegarth — except for you and your companions, I am the only living human being in this hotel," the voice goes on. "Whatever you do, don't go to sleep tonight. If you fall asleep, you'll turn into a ghost yourself! But I can help you. I've got the keys to the front door. Come find me. And hurry! I'm in Room —"

Before you can find out the room number, the voice breaks into a horrible scream.

Then the line goes dead.

Hang up, and turn to PAGE 75.

Oh, no! Are the skeletons coming to life?

Then you see a mouse creep out from under the pile of bones.

"Ohhh." You sigh in relief. The *mouse* made the bones move.

"Don't laugh," Moira begins slowly. "But I have a really weird idea. I think if I touch these bones, the dead people will talk to me. Maybe they'll tell us how to get out of here."

You glance at Moira sideways. Is she nuts?

"I know it sounds crazy," Moira tells you. "But I have the strangest feeling that it will work."

"Whatever." You shrug. Beats sitting around doing nothing.

Moira strolls over to the huge pile of skeletons. She hesitates a moment, then lays both hands on one of the skeletons.

"Listen!" she cries, her eyes wide. "Did you hear that?"

You shake your head.

"It's an old woman," Moira explains. "She said, 'Move the bones. There is a door behind.'"

A door? A way out? Hmmmm . . .

But are you going to take advice from a skeleton?

Maybe you should touch the bones yourself. See if *you* hear anything. . . .

If you do what Moira says, turn to PAGE 131.
If you want to touch the bones yourself, turn to PAGE 16.

Your mouth drops open as you stare at the ghost girl.

She looks about fourteen years old. Her long red hair is pulled back from her face with a black velvet band. She's wearing blue jeans and a blue sweatshirt.

"I'm Sara Ware," she tells you. She reaches out to touch your arm. You flinch and jump back.

Sara smiles. "Don't be afraid," she assures you. "I'm just like you. My family came here for a vacation last year — and the ghosts got us. Now I'm one of them. But not really. I hate this place. I don't want anyone else to turn into a ghost."

"You're not like us," Jamie blurts out. "You're a *ghost*."

You shudder and nod.

"I can't help that," Sara replies sadly. "But I *can* help *you*. All you have to do is come with me to my room on the fourth floor. I'll bring Drew Mortegarth to you. Trust me," she adds, holding out a hand toward you.

A cold current of air drifts toward you when she moves.

She seems so nice . . . so sincere. . . .

But should you really trust a ghost?

If you trust her, go to her room on PAGE 82.
If you don't trust her, turn to PAGE 47.

You tell Jamie what the voice on the phone said.

"It's definitely a trap," Jamie declares. "I changed my mind about leaving. Someone wants us out of this room. So we should stay and check it out."

"Deal," you reply.

You and Jamie quickly search the room. Nothing.

As you're turning to go, you notice a small refrigerator in the corner of the room. You stoop down and peer into it.

"Clam juice," you mutter. "It's full of clam juice!"

"Yuck!" Jamie makes gagging noises. "I *hate* clam juice."

"Me too," you comment, slamming the fridge shut. "Clam juice is sick. Who would drink it?"

Then you wonder. Maybe drinking clam juice is lucky somehow. Maybe it protects people from the ghosts.

Maybe it's how Drew Mortegarth has survived all this time!

If you drink some clam juice, turn to PAGE 107.

If you don't, hurry to the dining room on PAGE 130.

You follow Jamie through the silent, carpeted halls.

The old hotel gives you the creeps. It's too quiet, too big . . . and too filled with ghosts!

And you're starting to feel sleepy. You yawn and blink. Don't fall asleep, you urge yourself. You shudder, remembering Drew Mortegarth's warning. You've got to stay awake — or you'll wind up a permanent guest at this haunted hotel!

You and Jamie pause in a huge archway leading into the lobby. The place looks empty, but . . .

Was that the sound of a newspaper rustling?

You shiver, feeling almost certain that someone is nearby. But you can't see anything unusual.

Jamie doesn't seem to notice. "Listen," he whispers. "One of us has to act crazy, to get the desk clerk's attention. Then the other person can sneak behind the desk to steal the keys. Which do you want to do?"

If you want to be the one who acts crazy, turn to PAGE 88.

If you want to steal the keys, turn to PAGE 63.

The noonday sun streaks in through the double front doors.

"Where do you think *you're* going in such a hurry?" the desk clerk calls in a nasty tone of voice.

But you ignore him. You lunge at the front door, grab the handle, and pull.

Yes! It opens!

"We're free!" you cry. You race out of the hotel. Into the parking lot. Toward Mrs. Matson's car.

To your surprise, Mrs. Matson is already outside. She's sitting in the car with the motor running. Moira and B. J. are in the car too.

"Jump in!" she shouts, waving her arms frantically for you to hurry.

You glance over your shoulder, looking for Drew.

But he's not following you. He's standing back at the hotel, in the open doorway. Waving goodbye.

"Sweet dreams," Drew calls, smiling a sad smile. "Sweet dreams . . ."

With that, Mrs. Matson guns the engine and zooms away — leaving the Hotel Morte far behind.

Turn to PAGE 127.

"Yikes!" Jamie murmurs softly.

For a minute, the two of you stare at your headless friend.

Then, slowly, Moira's head becomes solid again.

"B-b-b-but how?" Jamie stammers. "I mean, what — what happened to you?"

Moira looks a little guilty and shrugs. "Oh, after you guys left our room, B. J. and I went back inside. We were hungry, so we ate the Sweet Dreams mints. That was it. The next thing I knew, I was . . . well, you know. Like this. B. J. too. But it's not so bad being a ghost," she adds. "It's pretty cool, really."

"Cool?" You raise one eyebrow. "More like totally *cold*."

Moira laughs. "Okay, so it's cold. So what? It's fun. We get to hide all over the hotel, and we can walk through walls and everything. You should try it. Come on — eat a Sweet Dreams mint, and you can be a ghost too."

"Huh?" Your eyes pop open wide. "Are you nuts?"

She reaches into her pocket and hands you a mint.

"Go on," Jamie taunts you. "Eat it and turn into a ghost. I dare you."

Well? You *always* take Jamie's dares. What about this one?

If you take the dare, turn to PAGE 36.
If you don't take the dare, turn to PAGE 100.

Drew Mortegarth shakes his head. "There's a way out of the hotel," he goes on. "At least, there *used* to be."

You perk up. "Really?" you ask. "Where? When?"

"In the old days," Drew answers. "Even after the ghosts came, we could always get out at checkout. At noon. The doors were locked the rest of the time. But at noon they would open automatically — for just one minute — and we could go out. I don't know why, but a few months ago it stopped working that way."

"Hey!" Jamie exclaims. "Maybe they changed the checkout time!"

Well? Did they?

If you've met the ancient ghost who smells so bad, you *might* know the truth. The ghosts *did* change the checkout time.

But what time did they change it to?

Check out the answer on PAGE 62.

A blast of freezing cold air drifts out at you from the meat locker.

"Hurry up," Moira urges. "I hear someone coming!"

"But why do we have to go in there?" Jamie asks.

From the squeak in his voice, you can tell he's as nervous as you are.

"Because there's a secret room behind this one," Moira explains impatiently. "See that door?" She points to a small wooden door on the far side of the meat locker. "That leads to Drew Mortegarth's room."

"Oh," Jamie agrees. "Okay."

Shivering, Jamie steps into the meat locker. So do you.

That's when you notice something.

There's no food in there.

"Hey — where's the meat?" you demand, staring at Moira with wide eyes.

Turn to PAGE 80.

"What are you doing?" Jamie shouts.

You don't answer him. You simply keep running. You leap over the fence into the field.

"Hey!" you shout, waving your arms at the cows. "Hey! Over here! Look at me!"

The cows don't budge. They don't even glance up. They just keep grazing, their heads low.

You race headlong toward the herd, waving your arms and yelling at the top of your lungs. The cows ignore you.

When you reach the cows, you keep running . . . running . . .

And run *straight through* them! Your body passes easily through the solid beasts . . . as if you don't exist!

"Oh, no!" you cry. That's what you were afraid of!

It wasn't a ghost truck that passed through you on the highway. It was a real truck. *You and Jamie* are the ghosts!

"What's going on?" Jamie calls. He sounds scared.

You sigh. You hate to do it. But sooner or later you're going to have to tell your best friend the truth — you've both come to a very bad

END.

You and Jamie will turn into ghosts if you fall asleep!

You run to the door. You fiddle with the knob, pushing the lock buttons and twisting with all your might.

"We're locked in!" you cry.

"Figures," Jamie mutters. "Keep your eyes open," he adds. "We've got to stay awake!"

But he yawns, tired because it's so late. You yawn too.

"Turn off the music," you order. "Let's get some light."

You hurry to turn up the dimmer switch on the lights.

Jamie races to the cassette player. He punches the button to turn off the tape. But an instant later, you hear a click.

The lullabies start playing again.

"Hey! What's going on?" Jamie demands.

The lights dim again. A chill runs up your back. Just like the chill you felt in the elevator.

You can feel a cold draft moving through the room.

"What's happening?" Jamie moans.

"Ghosts," you answer softly. "Either Sara came back . . . or we have new visitors!"

Don't go to sleep — at least not until you turn to PAGE 8.

"Forget about Room 402," you tell Jamie. "Forget about finding Drew Mortegarth. Let's just get out of here alive."

You pick up the phone and dial 911.

The phone rings once. Twice.

Five times.

Fifteen times.

This is ridiculous! "I can't believe 911 isn't answering," you mutter.

Finally you hang up.

An instant later, there's a knock on the door.

Uh-oh. Your throat tightens. Who could that be?

Jamie heads toward the door. "Don't open it!" you whisper.

Too late.

He unlocks the door and swings it open.

Weird. No one's there.

But a freezing cold blast of air sweeps into the room.

"Thanks for using the phone — and letting us know which room you were hiding in!" an invisible voice says.

Turn to PAGE 106.

"Room service sounds good," you agree, nodding at Jamie.

You grab the menu, then pick up the phone.

"Okay — who wants what?" you ask the other kids.

By the time you're done, you've ordered four cheeseburgers, three large fries, ice cream, a piece of chocolate cake, a shrimp cocktail for Moira, a pizza, and six sodas.

"My mom's going to kill us," B. J. moans.

"Where is she, anyway?" Jamie wonders. "She's been gone a long time."

A knock on the door startles you. You open it.

"Whoa!" you blurt out and jump backwards.

A room-service cart loaded with food nearly knocks you over as it rolls into your room. But no one is pushing the cart.

You glance out the door. The hall is empty.

The cart rolls gently into the room, then stops.

"Weird!" B. J. says, his voice shaking. "Who knocked? How did that cart get in here? What's going on?"

"Is it a trick?" Moira asks, coming for a closer look.

B. J. shakes his head in amazement. "It's as if the food was brought by ghosts!"

Turn to PAGE 65.

Already dead?

The words hit you like a punch in the gut.

The bus driver begins to fade into nothingness. Right before your eyes.

A moment ago he was a scrawny man with a tan, wrinkled face. A gray uniform. A gray cap.

Now he's . . . nothing. Gone. Vanished. A ghost.

"Enjoy your ride!" the ghost says, his voice drifting away.

"Where did he go?" Jamie cries, sounding panicked. "Is he still driving?"

You have no idea.

All you know is that the bus is speeding through the pitch-black night. Eighty miles an hour. Tearing down the highway. Screeching around curves.

Faster . . . faster . . .

"We have to take over the wheel!" Jamie shouts.

You'd better do it, you figure. You're closest to the driver's seat.

Can you really drive the bus? Find out on PAGE 128.

As soon as Jamie hears you, he runs from the lobby.

"Come on! To the elevator!" you call. You and Jamie race to the wood-paneled elevator at the back of the lobby. You dash in just as the desk clerk is about to catch up with you.

"Come back here, you little creeps!" the desk clerk shouts.

As the elevator doors close, the desk clerk sticks his hands in between them.

But the doors keep closing . . . closing. . . .

They smash shut on the man's hands.

"Yikes!" Jamie cries.

An instant later, the elevator starts to move up.

Ewww. Sick! you think. His hands will be torn off his arms!

But the clerk's hands suddenly turn airy and see-through. You stare at the ghostly forms. Then they disappear as the elevator rises, groaning and creaking, to the top floor.

When the doors open again, you gasp.

Guess who's standing there — waiting for you?

Turn to PAGE 77.

You run, following Moira's voice to the stair-well.

"Hellllp!" Her cries echo in the hollow space.

The sound is coming from below, you decide.

You race down the stairs. One flight. Another . . .

Finally you can't go down any farther. You push through a heavy wooden door into a dark, dank basement.

"What is *this*?" you mutter.

It takes a minute for your eyes to adjust to the dark.

Then you see them.

Bones.

Thousands and thousands of skeletons — all piled up in a twisting, cavernous, candlelit room!

Explore the basement on PAGE 11.

You decide to take Jamie's dare and become a ghost.

After all — you *always* take his dares. Don't you?

What are you — nuts?

You are going to become a ghost because someone *dared* you?

News flash: If you keep taking dangerous dares, you're not just going to die on *this* page.

You're going to bite the dust on every page of every GIVE YOURSELF GOOSEBUMPS book you ever read!

And that's no fun.

You want to *win* in this book, right? Get to the good endings. Beat the ghosts at their own game!

Of course you do.

So close the book, go lie down for a few minutes, and have a nice cold glass of lemonade.

Just cool out.

And don't you *dare* open this book again — until you're ready to make your own choices. No matter what Jamie dares you to do!

THE END

You drop down on all fours in front of the doggie door.

"You look stupid," Jamie teases you.

"I *feel* stupid," you admit.

But you push your head through the swinging rubber flap and crawl outside.

By the time you squeeze out, you're all scratched up. And sticky. Gross. The doggie door is glopped up with saliva from dogs licking it. And poking through with their noses.

But you don't care. At least you've escaped from the ghosts!

You stand up and glance around.

A moment later Jamie crawls out behind you. "Now what?" he asks, scrambling to his feet.

The two of you shiver as you gaze at the deserted road. It's a cold, moonlit night. And very clear. You can see that there is no traffic.

You turn to the woods behind the hotel. Gnarled, twisted trees loom in the moonlight.

You think you spot a faint light, way in the distance, through the woods. It could be a house.

"Well?" Jamie asks.

If you go toward the light in the woods, turn to PAGE 14.

If you go toward the road, turn to PAGE 58.

"Right!" you shout at Jamie. "There is a new checkout time! Remember? The old ghost told us. It's at eleven in the morning!"

"Really?" Drew stares at you. For just an instant, you see a flicker of light in his dark eyes.

You nod. "A creepy ancient ghost told us," you explain. "A guy who never washes. Or cuts his hair."

"Pee-yew!" Jamie adds, waving a hand in front of his nose.

"That's Grandpa," Drew murmurs, nodding.

"So what are we going to do?" Jamie asks. "Just hang out in this closet until eleven A.M.?"

Drew shrugs. "We have to. It's too dangerous to go roaming around the hotel. There's only one big problem."

"What?" You're not sure you really want an answer to your question.

"We'll only have one minute to get out," Drew says.

"So?" You sigh in relief. "We can make it from here to the front door easily in one minute."

"I know," Drew says impatiently. "But what if our watches are wrong?"

Turn to PAGE 122.

You shield your face with your arms. The ghosts whack you.

Then you hear Jamie calling from the elevator.

"Hey — enough of the monkey act!" he shouts. "Let's go. I've got the keys!"

"Monkey act? I'm not doing a monkey act, you moron!" you yell. "I'm trying to escape from these killer ghosts!"

You jerk your leg extra hard. The bony grip on your ankle loosens, and you leap off the couch. You dart toward the elevator.

"Good-bye and good riddance! And don't come back!" a ghost shouts after you. Jamie's eyes widen in fear.

"Don't worry — we won't!" you shout back.

"Wow — there really were ghosts in the lobby," Jamie says as you both start to step inside the elevator. "Let's go back to the room and find Moira and B. J."

A strange chill suddenly wafts across your shoulders.

Uh-oh. Did a ghost just brush by you to get into the elevator?

"M-maybe we should take the stairs," you suggest nervously.

"Up all those flights?" Jamie punches the button for your floor. "Are you nuts? Hurry, before those spooks in the lobby come after us."

If you get on the elevator, turn to PAGE 55.
If you take the stairs, turn to PAGE 81.

40

You're trapped. Buried under the pile of skeletons. Moira is too. You can't move. Neither of you can move an inch.

"Move the bones — there is a door behind," the old woman ghost chortles. "Ha-ha-ha! I can't believe you fell for it!"

Huh? The woman is repeating the words that Moira heard when she touched the bones!

"Oh, no," Moira moans. "I thought the *bones* were speaking. But it was her! That ghost!"

"Thanks for the help, dearie," the old woman says. "Now we're free!"

"Free?" Moira repeats.

"Yes," the old woman replies. "None of us spirits can ever leave this hotel — unless we find someone to replace us. Now we have. You two will take our places — forever."

With that, she floats over to a wooden door.

A door that *was* hidden behind the pile of skeletons.

She lifts the latch and flings open the creaky door. She and the boy float out of the hotel. You strain to follow.

"Good-bye, my dears," she calls. "And happy haunting!"

THE END

"The seventh dwarf is Sneaky," you announce firmly.

"Sneaky," the ghost repeats, as if he's memorizing the name.

He nods and lets out a tremendous sigh of relief. The sigh sends another cold blast of air your way. Not only does this ghost smell, he has bad breath too!

You and Jamie exchange worried glances.

Sneaky? Was that right? It doesn't sound exactly right. . . .

Because it isn't!

But the ancient ghost falls for it. What does he know? He hasn't been to a movie in eighty years!

"All right," the ghost moans. "Sleepy, Dopey, Doc, Grumpy, Happy, Sneezy, and Sneaky. I will keep my eye out for them. Dwarfs are very dangerous."

He moves toward the door. "And I will keep my promise to you too. I will let you live. Come. There is an exit that only I know about. It's in the Bat's Ballroom!"

Follow him to the Bat's Ballroom on PAGE 6.

You decide to go to Room 402.

But first you finish reading the brochure. It's all about the seven members of the Mortegarth family. And how six of them died strange, violent deaths.

All in Room 402!

"Weird," you comment, tossing the brochure back to Jamie. "But I bet you're right. Room 402 must be Drew Mortegarth's room."

The two of you hurry through the hotel till you find it. It's on the fourth floor. You use your master key to unlock it. Then you step in.

"Whoa!" Jamie gasps, jumping back almost at once.

You gulp. Your stomach turns over. You want to scream.

Get a grip, and turn to PAGE 132.

You can't believe your eyes.

A fat lady. A lion tamer with DIETRICH THE GREAT written in sequins on his shirt. Two women bareback riders. The Flying Watusis, a famous trapeze act.

A man in the front seat is swallowing fire. His son, beside him, is swallowing a sword.

"Cool!" Jamie exclaims. "What are you doing on the bus?"

A man dressed as a ringmaster stands up. "This is our tour bus," he explains. "We're doing a road tour for a three-ring circus. Too bad we only play for *dead* audiences."

Huh? Does he mean they only play for *ghosts*?

You don't even care! You're just happy to be hanging out with so many interesting people. This is too cool to be true.

"That bus driver was crazy," the lion tamer mutters from the back. "We need someone new to drive. I say let those kids do it."

And that's just what happens.

You and Jamie spend the rest of your lives driving the bus for a circus act called THE GREATEST GHOSTS ON EARTH!

THE END

"I'm up for a movie," you declare. "What's on?"

"Let's find out," B. J. answers, flipping channels.

"Welcome to the Hotel Morte," a ghoulish-looking man on the screen announces. "We're glad you tuned in to the hotel channel. We always like to welcome our guests. Watch carefully, now," he adds in a deep, creepy voice.

The man's face suddenly becomes pale and transparent — like a ghost. Then he lifts his wispy, filmy arm toward you.

He reaches straight *through* the television screen!

Yikes! Turn to PAGE 135.

Desperately, you yank on the door handle one more time.

Then you notice the sign on the glass:

PLEASE USE OTHER DOOR.

There are two big glass doors at the front of the hotel. One of them is still locked. But the other . . .

You shift sideways and grab the other door handle.

"Yes!" you cry as the door pulls open.

B. J. and Moira race through the lobby. Out the front door. Into the sunlight.

Down the steps to the empty parking lot.

B. J.'s mother is right behind them.

But so are the ghosts!

You start to slam the door shut behind Mrs. Matson.

That's when you see Jamie and Drew Mortegarth. They pop out from behind a marble pillar in the lobby. They race toward you.

"Hold it open!" Jamie begs as they dash for the front door.

Oh, no! you think. Your heart leaps into your throat.

If you hold the door open, the ghosts will come out too.

And you don't know *what* they're capable of!

Turn to PAGE 109.

46

"Don't go in there!" Jamie cries. Fear chokes his voice.

For a moment, you stare in horror.

The bloodstain spreads even more, creeping toward you.

Then a wall starts bleeding! As if it's telling you that someone died with his blood splattered all over it.

A moment later, the moaning starts. You hear a hundred voices wailing . . . as if calling to you from their graves.

"Go away!" the voices cry. "Awaaaaaay!"

"Let's get out of here," Jamie urges you.

You want to run — you really do.

But the room holds you there. It seems to have some power over you. Making you stay.

A minute later, the voices stop moaning. The walls stop bleeding. The stain on the floor disappears.

Turn to PAGE 89.

The girl ghost gives you a horrible chill.

"No thanks. I *don't* trust you!" you tell her. You quickly push the button for the nearest floor.

The doors open on the second floor. You dash out.

But Jamie doesn't follow.

"Where are you going?" he calls, still standing in the elevator with Sara.

Before you can answer, the doors close again.

Oh, well, you think. Maybe she'll take Jamie to Drew Mortegarth.

But your instincts told you to get out of there — fast!

You gaze up and down the hallway.

Now what?

Faintly, in the distance, you hear voices. Coming from the stairwell. Then a high-pitched cry.

It sounds exactly like Moira!

"Helllllp!" she screams. "Somebody — help!"

See if you can find her on PAGE 35.

48

You lunge for the doorknob and turn it.

To your surprise, it opens easily.

"Go on," the ghost shouts, following you to the door. "Leave this room if you wish! But you cannot leave the hotel."

"What's going to stop us?" you demand.

"It's nearly one A.M.," the ghost declares. Then he lowers his voice, as if he's telling you a secret. "Checkout time is eleven o'clock in the morning. You see?"

"No," you reply, feeling confused. "I don't see."

The ghost lowers his voice even more.

"The doors of the hotel unlock automatically each day. But only at eleven A.M. They remain unlocked for just one minute. You can check out tomorrow morning at eleven o' clock. If you live that long!"

With that, the old ghost suddenly becomes transparent — and floats right *through* you!

Turn to PAGE 102.

You, Jamie, Moira, and B. J. stare at the TV in shock.

"Don't try to escape," the ghost on the TV continues. "The doors are all locked. There's no way out. And everyone you'll meet here — every single one of our guests and staff — is a ghost!"

B. J. gasps. "Help!" he wails. "Mom!"

The ghost chuckles. "Oh, we'll be taking care of *her*."

"Wow," Jamie murmurs.

"Good night, now," the ghost adds. "And sweet dreams . . ."

Sweet dreams?

When he says those words, you glance toward the bed.

Hey!

SWEET DREAMS . . . FROM HOTEL MORTE.

That's what's printed on the wrappers of the four little mints. The mints that are resting on the bed pillows.

You hurry to the bed and pick up a mint. "Look," you announce. "Sweet dreams. That's what the ghost said. And it says the same thing on the wrapper!"

"Don't eat it," Moira warns quickly. "I'll bet it's poison. The mints will probably kill us. Or maybe just put us to sleep — forever!"

Turn to PAGE 68.

Moira, B. J., and Mrs. Matson follow as you race toward the stairs. It seems like the best way to go. If you wait for the elevator, you'll never make it in time.

But the instant you step into the stairwell, you scream.

"Aaahhhhhhh!"

The stairs are *filled* with ghosts! Some of them have huge dark circles around their eyes and chalk-white skin. Others look normal. Some are just shadows of human beings.

The chill in the air is awful. Almost like a freezer.

They call to you. "Stayyyyy with us," they cry.

"Sleeeep!" a few ghosts moan. "Sleeeeep tonight and become our friends!"

Your heart pounds in terror as the ghosts reach out for you. Their hands paw the air, trying to grab you.

If you go up the stairs, you'll have to push through the crowd. Against their cold bodies . . .

But you've got to get up to the first floor — and fast! You've only got two minutes left! Well?

If you push your way through the ghosts, turn to PAGE 113.

If you take the elevator instead, turn to PAGE 67.

You decide to sing songs to stay awake.

You and Jamie start with your favorite rap songs. Then you sing camp songs and Christmas carols. You harmonize perfectly.

You're having so much fun, you forget all about the ghosts. And the haunted hotel.

Until you hear a third voice joining in. . . .

You shudder. Oh, no!

You're not alone!

Who's there? Find out on PAGE 69.

Jamie stares at you, his eyes drilling into yours.

"Eat the mint. I *double* dare you!" he taunts.

This is stupid, you think as you unwrap the mint. But you can't help it. Jamie has a way of making you act like a jerk.

You pop the chocolate candy into your mouth and chew.

"Ummm," you say, your mouth full.

A moment later, your eyes close. Your head feels dizzy. Then you slump to the floor in a twisted heap.

Oh, no! Will "ummmm" really be your last word on earth?

Turn to PAGE 78.

For an instant, you think you're going to suffocate.

Then the gas in the room begins to clear.

And you see what *else* is escaping from the cola can.

A young woman! A totally cool-looking girl with spiky red and purple hair. And five earrings.

She's wearing a fuzzy black sweater, baggy blue jeans, and combat boots.

"Hi, kiddoes!" She snaps her gum and grins at you. "Guess what? You're in the wrong book!"

Huh?

Turn to PAGE 133 in this book.

B. J. joins you in the bathroom. "We're *all* going to die," he moans.

"That's right," a spooky voice says, coming from nowhere. "You're going to end up just like meeeeee. . . ."

The voice trails off. But a moment later, a wispy form appears in the room. He's wearing a waiter's uniform and carrying a white towel.

You can see right through him!

"Yikes!" Jamie cries. "A ghost!"

"Yes," the ghostly waiter replies. "I am a ghost. And you will be too. Very soon."

"The food," Moira wails. "It must have been poisoned!"

"Not poisoned," the ghost corrects her. "Let's just say it was spiced — with our special ingredients. They'll turn you into ghosts by morning. I'm afraid you're going to feel a tiny bit sick for a few hours, first, however."

You close your eyes and wish you could barf.

"I *knew* we should have watched a pay-per-view movie instead," B. J. complains. "I don't want to be a ghost!"

"Oh, quit your whining," the ghost scolds. "Just be glad no one ordered the Seizure Salad!"

THE END

You dash into the elevator just as the doors slide shut.

"Phew, that was close," Jamie comments. He slumps against the wall. "But it was worth it."

"Uh-huh," you reply absently. You can't shake the feeling that you and Jamie aren't the only ones going up.

Then you feel it again — that sudden coldness. As if an icy hand clutched your shoulder.

And do you hear something . . . ?

Find out on PAGE 66.

56

You think hard, trying to figure out which person is Drew Mortegarth.

Your life might depend on getting this right.

Your head pounds. Is it the kid? Or the woman in the red dress?

Wait a minute . . .

Maybe you already *know* the answer!

Did you look inside the refrigerator in Room 402? If so, you know what Drew Mortegarth likes to drink.

Your eyes light up. You gaze at the blond woman. "What's your favorite drink?" you ask her, eyeing her carefully.

"My favorite drink?" she repeats, frowning. "Cola. Why?"

You turn to the kid. "How about yours?" you ask him.

"Clam juice," the kid replies. "What a weird question."

Well?

Which do you think it is?

If you think Drew likes cola, turn to PAGE 91.
If you think Drew likes clam juice, turn to PAGE 13.

"Yes," Moira replies proudly. "I found Drew Mortegarth. He's a kid like us. The last of the Mortegarth family. He lives in a secret room on the first floor."

"Wow!" Jamie exclaims. "How did you find him?"

"B. J. and I were trying to hide from the ghosts," Moira explains. "So we sneaked into the kitchen, and we found a secret room behind the freezer. Come on — I'll show you. You have to go through the meat locker to get there."

You and Jamie follow Moira out of the room.

"That explains it," Jamie comments as you reach the hall.

"Explains what?" Moira asks.

"Why you're so cold," Jamie replies. "I mean, there's a chill in the air around you — just like around the ghosts."

Your stomach does a double flip.

Just like the ghosts?

Oh, no! What if the ghosts already got to Moira? Then she'd be . . .

Uh-oh.

Is she one of them?

If you trust Moira, turn to PAGE 84.
If you think she's a ghost, turn to PAGE 126.

No way are you going into those dark woods, you decide.

You rub your arms to stay warm. Then you slowly walk toward the road.

"Hey," Jamie calls as the two of you reach the front parking lot. "Look! A bus!"

He's right. Parked next to Mrs. Matson's car in the empty parking lot is a big silver tour bus. It's empty, except for a driver who seems to be snoozing at the wheel.

"Cool!" Jamie cries. "This is our ticket out of here!"

Jamie races ahead of you and climbs on the bus. You run to catch up. You leap onto the steps, joining Jamie inside.

The instant you are in the bus — too far inside to be able to leave — the bus driver awakens.

He pulls a lever, closing the bus door.

"Where to, chums?" the driver asks. He tips his hat at you with a grin.

But before you can answer, he jerks the bus into gear. Then he speeds out of the parking lot and into the night.

Find out where you're going on PAGE 4.

You cross your fingers for good luck and blurt out the answer.

"Bashful!" you announce. "The seventh dwarf is Bashful!"

The old ghost closes his wrinkled eyelids for a moment.

"Yesssss . . . ," he declares finally, nodding. "That must be true. I sense it."

"All right!" Jamie shouts, giving you a high five.

"Now let us out." You don't think you can stand the ghost's awful smell another moment. You dart for the door. "We're going to find our other friends. We want to leave."

"No!" the ghost booms. "I promised to let you *live*. I didn't say you could *leave*!"

Turn to PAGE 48.

"It's the phone number," Jamie announces with a sneaky grin. "Of the hotel where the rest of our class is staying in D.C."

"So?" you ask, still bewildered.

"So I say we call them," he replies. "Call the other parents. And our teachers. Tell them we need help. Tell them B. J.'s mom disappeared — and that they'd better all come here right away to help us!"

"But then they'll get trapped here too," you respond slowly. "They'll all become ghosts. Like us."

A huge grin spreads across Jamie's face.

"I know," he admits. "But that way we'll have friends. We'll never be lonely again!"

He pauses. "I dare you," he finally adds.

So of course you do it. After all — you can't resist Jamie's dares!

THE END

You hold your breath, waiting.

Waiting for the ghost to fling the bat in your face!

CLICK.

A bright light flashes in your eyes. You squint, blinded by the sudden glare.

Then you almost laugh. It wasn't a bat, you realize. It was a *lightbulb* — hanging from the ceiling!

The old ghost pulled a chain and turned it on.

Now, in the light, you can see the door at the far end of the hallway. Straight ahead.

"This way out," the ghost announces. He turns the knob and opens the door.

"Yes!" you cry.

Just beyond the door lies the clear, cold night air. A million stars twinkle in the inky sky.

"We're out of here!" Jamie exclaims, dashing out the door.

But you don't follow him. Jamie turns and stares at you.

"What are you waiting for?" he demands.

You stare back at Jamie, not moving an inch.

Answer Jamie on PAGE 129.

No cheating.

Did you meet the smelly old ghost? If so, did he tell you what the new checkout time is?

If you *do* know the new checkout time, write the number down.

Add twenty-seven to the number.

You will have a two-digit number.

Turn to the page that is the same as that number. Remember, it's the new checkout time, plus twenty-seven.

If you know the new number, turn to that page now.

If you don't know the new checkout time, turn to PAGE 85.

"I'll try to steal the keys," you tell Jamie. "You do something crazy in the lobby."

"Okay," Jamie agrees, his eyes lighting up.

Before you know it, he's off. He dashes into the lobby and starts shouting at the top of his lungs.

"Peanuts! Hot dogs! Get your nice hot peanuts here!"

In a flash, the desk clerk is out from behind his desk.

"Hey — you can't sell peanuts here," he says. "You don't have a license!"

A license? Too weird! you think. But as the clerk charges in Jamie's direction, you slip behind the desk.

Keys. There must be keys somewhere here. . . .

You scan the old-fashioned cubbyholes on the wall where the keys should be. They're empty.

Then you spot a large brass key on a ring. You grab it. Maybe it's the master key. The one that will open all the rooms.

"I've got it!" you call to Jamie.

Take the key, and run to PAGE 34.

"No, wait," B. J. cries. "You guys can't *leave* us here."

Typical B. J., you think. He's kind of a wimp.

"We're not leaving you, dodo," Jamie says. "We're *all* going. We'll split up and search the hotel. Then we'll meet back here in an hour. Exactly at midnight. If we've found Drew Mortegarth and the key — great. If not, we'll make another plan. Okay?"

You nod and Moira shrugs. But B. J. looks worried as he follows the three of you to the door.

You step into the hall. Then you push the button for the elevator — just as the elevator doors open.

Inside, you see something airy. A filmy form of some sort.

It moves slowly . . . toward you. . . .

It's a ghost, larger than any human being you've ever seen!

Face your first real ghost on PAGE 92.

Moira's mouth drops open as she watches the door to your room close by itself.

"Maybe the hotel is haunted," she whispers. "You know. Just like you said. Hotel Morte means Dead Hotel — right? Maybe there's a ghost in here — right now!"

You nod silently and gaze around the room.

"Don't be dumb," Jamie scoffs. "They're probably really busy in the kitchen right now. They use remote-controlled carts or something. Maybe the cart is programmed to come here and —"

"And *knock* on the door?" B. J. interrupts.

"B. J.'s got a point," you admit. "But I don't see any ghosts. And I'm starved!"

So is everyone else. The four of you dig in. You devour the burgers, fries, cake, colas, and everything else.

And within an hour . . . you're all sick as dogs!

You feel wretched. You break out in a cold sweat. You rush to the bathroom to throw up, but you can't.

"I feel like I'm going to die!" Moira moans.

"Me too," you groan, barely able to get the words out.

Turn to PAGE 54.

You glance around nervously. The only other person you see is Jamie. But you know by now that just because you can't see somebody doesn't mean they aren't there!

You freeze when you hear a faint sound.

SSSSSSS.

You hold your breath and stare wide-eyed at Jamie.

"Hear that?" you whisper.

Jamie nods.

You both listen carefully to the hissing sound. It sounds like someone breathing in and out through their nose. But the nose is stopped up, so it's whistling.

"Where is it?" Jamie whispers.

Before you can answer, a ghost materializes in the elevator near the control panel.

"I'm here." The airy image of a teenage girl smiles at you. "And if you do what I say, I'll lead you to Drew Mortegarth."

Hear the ghost's instructions on PAGE 22.

"Run for the elevator!" you cry, whirling around.

You lead the way through the basement, toward the one old elevator in the hotel. You push the button frantically.

You glance up at the dial above the elevator door. It shows what floor the elevator is on.

"Oh, no," Moira cries. "We blew it! The elevator is on the thirteenth floor . . . and it's going up!"

Oh, well. Moira's right. You gambled — and you lost.

By the time the elevator reaches the basement, it's long past eleven A.M. Long past checkout time.

But it's not too late for *you* to check out . . .

As in "so long." "Good-bye."

You're a goner.

You've checked out — for good!

THE END

Jamie twists his mouth into a sneer. "Don't be ridiculous," he scolds Moira. "You're afraid of a *mint?*"

He marches to the bed and grabs a mint. He reads the words on the wrapper. "It's just candy," he insists. Then he tosses it to you. "Here — catch. Eat it. I dare you."

You stare at the green foil-wrapped mint in your hand. Why would I take this dare? you wonder.

Easy answer: You *always* take Jamie's dares. You can't resist!

But before you can unwrap the mint, the phone rings.

Wait a minute, you think. Who could be calling you *here*?

No one knows that the car broke down. No one knows you're at the Hotel Morte. . . .

Weird.

So what are you going to do? Eat the mint or answer the phone?

If you answer the phone, turn to PAGE 20.
If you eat the mint, turn to PAGE 52.

"Jin-gle bells . . . jin-gle bells," the mysterious voice sings.

Your heart thuds. Jamie stops singing and whirls around.

"Who was that?" Jamie gasps.

In answer, a form begins to appear in the room.

You blink, amazed at how alive — how *normal* — the ghost seems when he becomes solid.

It's a man in a fancy gray suit, blue shirt, and silk tie. He's about your dad's age. And he looks familiar.

Have you seen him on television or something?

He holds out his hand.

"Shake, kid." He greets you in a friendly voice. "I'm Sandy Brecker. Remember me? Host of *Top Talent Review*?"

"Yeah!" You snap your fingers. "That TV show!"

"Right you are." Sandy Brecker grins at you. "America's number-one-rated talent search show. If there's one thing I know, it's talent — and you kids have it!"

Huh?

Turn to PAGE 95.

"What's in there?" you ask, your voice shaking.

"Nothing," the hideous ghost answers impatiently. "It's just a hall leading to an exit. Hurry! Go on!"

"You go first," Jamie urges you. "I dare you."

Trembling, you step into the dark hallway and glance up.

You notice a small dark shape hanging upside down from the ceiling.

Your skin starts to crawl. You have a horrible feeling that you know what it is.

A bat. Maybe even a vampire bat!

The old ghost hurries ahead of you. He reaches up and touches the thing on the ceiling.

Yuck, you think. Did he just grab that bat?

What's he going to *do* with it, anyway?

Find out on PAGE 61.

The invisible ghost grabs your ankle with both hands. He shakes your leg, trying to make you fall. Then he starts biting!

"Ouch! Oww-oww!" you shriek as you feel the invisible teeth sink into your calf.

Across the lobby, you can hear Jamie laughing. "Great job," he whispers loudly. "Great monkey. Keep it up!"

"I'm not being a monkey," you call to Jamie from the couch. "Someone's biting me!"

But when you glance over your shoulder, Jamie has vanished!

What did he do? you wonder. Leave?

Turn to PAGE 112.

You fall sixteen floors — all the way from the top of the hotel to the basement — and land with a crunch.

For an instant you lie on the floor, dazed.

What happened?

The doors opened, you ran in, and then . . .

Oh, yeah. Now you remember. The elevator wasn't there!

You and Jamie leaped into the pitch-black elevator shaft!

Weird, you think. How come it didn't hurt more when you fell?

Jamie mumbles something and lifts his head from the floor.

"What did you say?" you ask him.

"I said I'm cold," Jamie repeats. "Freezing cold."

You squint at him in the dim light of the basement. You can see just the faintest outline of his head. Shoulders. Body.

You start to panic.

Did he say cold?

You're shivering yourself. You glance down at your own arms and legs.

You can barely see them.

They're transparent!

See if you show up on PAGE 12.

"Let's lie low back at the room," you suggest. "I think it will be safer."

You and Jamie head back to lie low.

Ooops. Lie low. Unfortunate choice of words.

You should never lie down when you're so tired. If you want to stay awake, that is.

After sleeping soundly for five full minutes, you and Jamie turn into ghosts yourselves!

Ah, well. You didn't think you were going to make it through this book just because you could name the Seven Dwarfs, did you?

No way. You'll have to go back and try again. But at least next time you'll have an important clue. Checkout time is eleven A.M. at the Hotel Morte!

THE END

74

So you know how to swim, do you?
Great.
But don't kid yourself.
Where you're going, swimming won't help.

Take a dive on PAGE 119.

Your eyes grow wide. You stand there listening to the dial tone like an idiot. Finally you hang up.

"Who was it?" Jamie demands.

"I don't know," you answer blankly. "Someone named Drew Mortegarth. He said he was the only human alive in the hotel. If he is a he," you add, remembering the strange voice.

"You don't know if you were talking to a guy or a girl?" Moira asks.

You shake your head. "The person whispered. I couldn't tell. But whoever it was warned us not to fall asleep — or we'll turn into ghosts."

"Ghosts?" B. J. repeats. His voice quavers with fear.

"Cool!" Jamie exclaims. "This place is awesome!"

"Drew promised to help," you continue. "He said —"

"Or *she* said," Moira cuts in.

"He said he —" You glance at Moira. "Or *she* — had keys. But before he — or she — could tell me what room to go to, I heard a scream, and the line went dead."

"So what are we waiting for?" Jamie exclaims, his eyes lighting up. "Let's go find this sucker!"

Turn to PAGE 64.

You glance back — and scream.

The halls of the hotel are crowded. Filled with hideous ghosts. Ghosts with no faces. Ghosts with skin falling off. All moaning, roaring, screaming as they come after you.

Your heart pounds in terror. You can barely breathe.

"Come on!" Sandy yells, stepping through the broken glass.

You and Jamie follow him outside. You race around to the back of the hotel. To an old convertible parked in the lot.

You all climb into the car, and Sandy starts the motor. You can't figure out how he did it, since he doesn't have a key.

Then he zooms down the road, barreling into the night.

Turn to PAGE 87.

The desk clerk faces you, solid as a living human being. Blocking your way out of the elevator.

His beady eyes glow. He snarls with anger.

Your eye is caught by the name tag on his white shirt: HORNER SMITHFIELD.

"I knew you were a ghost!" Jamie cries.

You nod. Horner Smithfield *must* be a ghost. How else could his hands have disappeared? How else could he zoom from the first floor to the fifteenth — and arrive before the elevator?

The desk clerk reaches toward you as if he's going to strangle you.

You glance at his hands. Your stomach flips over.

His hands aren't solid flesh. And they aren't transparent anymore.

They're . . . gone!

Turn to PAGE 86.

Well, it's certainly your last word on earth — as a *person*. But thanks to that Sweet Dreams mint, you can look forward to your first word on earth — as a ghost!

But don't be too upset. You manage to get back at the creeps who turned you into a ghost in the first place. You play so many practical jokes on the regular ghosts that they decide to haunt some other hotel!

In fact, because of your pranks, the Hotel Morte becomes a big tourist attraction. Jamie, Moira, and B. J. get summer jobs working at the hotel, so you can all hang out.

Yup! Being a ghost doesn't turn out to be so bad in

THE END.

"We can't leave," you tell Jamie. "We've got to help Moira and B. J. and his mom get out of here alive."

Jamie rolls his eyes in disgust. But finally he comes back into the hotel.

"All right," he agrees. "Let's go find Drew Mortegarth."

The ghost slowly shakes his head too. His rotting flesh flaps on his bones. "Drew Mortegarth cannot help you," he tells you. "Before the night is over, you will all die!"

He fades. His transparent form vanishes through the wall. The only thing he leaves behind is a faint bad smell.

"I'm a jerk for going along with this," Jamie mutters. But he marches down the hall back to the Bat's Ballroom.

You check your watch. "It's almost midnight. Let's go back to our room and see if Moira and B. J. are there. Maybe *they* found Drew Mortegarth."

"Fat chance," Jamie mumbles as he follows you through the empty, spooky hotel.

Turn to PAGE 81.

Moira smiles at you strangely. But she doesn't answer your question.

Instead, she pulls the door to the meat locker closed.

Locking all three of you in.

"What did you do that for?" Jamie shouts, horrified.

You study the huge metal door. Your heart sinks. There's no handle on the inside!

No way to open it. No way out.

"Now we're trapped in here!" you moan.

"No," Moira says slyly. "*We're* not trapped in here. *You* are. Bye-bye."

All at once she becomes transparent.

Thin and airy and filmlike.

"Oh, no!" Jamie cries. "She's . . . she's a ghost!"

I knew it! you want to yell.

But before you can even open your mouth, Moira floats through the metal door. Leaving you and Jamie shivering.

And locked inside!

Hurry to PAGE 103 before you freeze.

There's no sign of Moira or B. J. back at your room.

"Now what?" you mutter.

"Don't worry," Jamie tells you. "We still have our original plan." He dangles the desk clerk's key ring in front of you.

"Let's get started checking all the rooms in the hotel," he suggests.

"Great —" you start to say.

But you stop speaking when you notice the bedspread moving.

By itself!

It starts to wrinkle, just a little. As if someone is sitting on it. Scooting around. Then the spread lifts off the bed and starts flapping slowly in your direction.

A ghost, you realize with a gulp.

And it's getting closer.

You turn around. Jamie's eyes are open wide as he stares at the floating bedspread.

"What should we do?" he mouths.

What will you do? Find out on PAGE 96.

You decide to trust Sara. You push the button for the fourth floor and follow her to Room 444.

When you reach the room, Sara floats right through the wooden door. A moment later, she opens the door from inside. She's still transparent and ghostly.

"Come on in and get comfortable," she offers.

"Wow!" Jamie murmurs, eyeing her room.

"Yikes," you add softly.

The room gives you the creeps.

The whole place is filled with cushions, mattresses, and pillows piled up on the floor. There is no dresser. No table.

There isn't even any space to walk.

Just looking at it makes you sleepy.

"What a great place for a pillow fight. Or a sleep-over party," Jamie declares.

"Yeah," you agree weakly. "There's only one problem. We're not supposed to go to sleep! Remember? Because if we do, we'll turn into ghosts!"

Keep your eyes open and turn to PAGE 101.

You yank open the broom closet door.

"Yaaiiii!" you scream, shocked by what you see.

There, in the closet, are the ghostly relatives of Drew Mortegarth. The whole Mortegarth family!

A thin line of blood circles the neck of the old man — Grandpa. It stains the shirt near the heart of a woman.

The ghosts lunge at you, moaning. "Staaaayyy with us," they cry, reaching for you.

"No!" you shout, backing up. "Where's Jamie? Where's Drew?"

"Helllp!" Moira screams at the top of her lungs.

A cry of terror escapes from B. J.'s mom too.

"We've got to find Jamie!" you yell frantically.

"We can't!" B. J. calls. "It's almost 11:01!"

No, you think. No! You can't miss your chance to escape.

In a panic, you run across the slippery marble floor of the lobby, toward the front door.

You yank on the door handle.

"Open it!" B. J. cries.

You jerk your arm hard, trying to pull open the front door.

But it's locked.

"No!" you shout. "Please! Let us out!"

Turn to PAGE 45.

You decide to trust Moira.

She doesn't seem like a ghost. Besides, meat lockers *are* cold. . . .

"We can't take the elevator," Moira declares, leading you to a stairway. "Drew told us to stay away from it. The ghosts are always in there — even if you can't see them."

"Where's B. J.?" you ask her.

"He's with Drew," Moira replies. "He was too chicken to come looking for you guys, so I came alone."

Typical B. J., you think.

The three of you hurry down a back stairway to the first floor. Then Moira leads you to a set of swinging double doors. They lead into the old hotel kitchen.

The kitchen is empty, except for a bunch of giant pots and pans. You shudder when you spot the glistening knives and meat cleavers hanging from a rack on one wall.

You follow Moira toward a thick steel door with a big handle. It's a big walk-in refrigerator. Or meat locker. Moira opens the door and motions for you to go in.

"After you," she says.

Enter the meat locker on PAGE 28.

"Maybe there's a new checkout time," you tell Jamie. "But we don't know what it is. I say we go with the old one."

"Huh?" Jamie grunts. "Why? Drew just told us it won't work."

"It doesn't work for *him*," you point out. "But maybe it will work for us. Maybe the doors will open!"

Jamie nods and shrugs. "Worth a try," he says.

The three of you decide to hide in the broom closet until a few minutes before noon. Then you and Jamie creep out.

You sneak into the lobby and crouch behind a chair — although there's no reason to hide. The lobby seems to be empty.

Drew squats down beside you.

"It's one minute till noon," Drew murmurs.

Silently, the three of you count to sixty.

"Get ready," you whisper. "Get set . . . go!"

Your blood pumps wildly as you jump up and dash past the desk clerk — racing for the front door!

Don't stop running until you get to PAGE 25.

At the end of Horner Smithfield's shirtsleeves there is . . .

Nothing.

No hands. No stumps. Just *nothing*.

"You'll never get out of here alive!" he threatens.

"How are you going to stop us?" Jamie jeers. "You seem to be a little shorthanded!"

How can Jamie make jokes at a time like this? You're so scared, your legs tremble.

Smithfield glares at Jamie. "You'll be sorry," he warns.

With that, the five strands of hair on his bald head rise.

They lift up off his scalp. And point at *you*!

Hey! I thought *Jamie* was the one who was supposed to be sorry, you think. Not *me*!

You stare in horror at the five solid, sharp spikes attached to Horner Smithfield's head.

They're alive!

They seem to grow longer. Sharper. They look like the teeth of a pitchfork. But they move like snakes.

They aim at your face — as if they're going to poke out your eyes.

Duck to PAGE 116.

Seven hours later, you arrive in New York. It's early morning, and the whole city is bustling with traffic.

Sandy parks the car, then takes you to the offices of his old television show. He introduces you to a guy named Mel Morgan, a record producer.

"These kids have real talent," he tells Mel.

"Fine, fine," Mel says. "I'll give them a deal. But, Sandy — where have you been for the past year? You just disappeared!"

Sandy gives you a private nod — as if to say, "Don't give away my secret." Then he turns to Mel. "Yeah, I disappeared," he says. "And that's what I've got to do again."

A moment later, he's gone.

You never see Sandy again. But you do become famous singers — based on your hit country song called "You Thought You Gave Me Goosebumps, But It Was Only Fleas!"

THE END

"I'll act crazy," you answer. "But what should I do?"

"Run in there and start jumping all over the furniture," Jamie suggests with a laugh. "Make sounds like a monkey. That'll be soooo funny!"

"Okay," you agree. It's a good plan. And it might even be fun.

You pause in the archway a minute more, listening. Was that a newspaper again? You could have sworn you heard pages turning.

"What are you waiting for?" Jamie whispers.

You shrug. "Here goes."

You race into the lobby, hunched over, dangling your arms like an ape. Then you leap up onto a leather couch.

"Hey!" someone shouts.

"Yeoowww!" you cry as you land on something lumpy.

Something bony.

Something alive!

You can't see anyone. But someone is definitely sitting on the couch.

And you just jumped on him!

Turn to PAGE 71.

You stand in the doorway to Room 402. It looks perfectly normal again. No blood on the floor. No stains on the wall.

Nothing.

Jamie gapes at you, totally freaked out. "What just happened?" he whispers.

"I don't know," you answer. "Maybe the spirits who died in this room are still here. Maybe they were warning us. To leave."

"Let's take their advice," Jamie says quickly. "Come on. That Drew Mortegarth person isn't here anyway."

"But maybe there are some clues here —" you start.

Then the phone rings.

You gulp. And slowly step into the room to answer it.

"Hello?" You're so nervous your voice squeaks.

"This is Drew Mortegarth," a voice on the other end whispers. "Come to the dining room. I'm waiting for you."

Then — *CLICK*.

The line goes dead.

Is this a trap?

Or should you do what the voice on the phone said?

Hurry to the dining room on PAGE 130.
Explore Room 402 further on PAGE 23.

"Don't trust her!" you shout at Jamie. "She's a ghost! I know it!"

"No way!" Jamie shakes his head.

But to your amazement, Moira smiles and nods.

"Okay, it's true," she admits, flipping her red hair off her shoulders with her hands. "I am a ghost. Watch."

When you see what she does next, your mouth falls open.

Little by little, her head begins to fade. Into nothingness! It totally disappears!

Moira twirls in a circle in the hallway.

Headless.

"Pretty cool, huh?" she declares, although you can't see her mouth. Or any part of her head.

Close your mouth, quit staring, and turn to PAGE 26.

"You like cola?" you repeat to the woman in the red dress.

You cross your fingers, hoping you've picked the right person. Hoping she's Drew Mortegarth.

She nods and smiles. Then she stands up and strolls to the back of the dining room. To a bar. She reaches into a small refrigerator and pulls out a can of cola.

"Would you like some?" she asks.

"Uh, sure," you answer. Then you remember — it's not smart to eat or drink *anything* in this hotel. "Uh, I mean, no!" You change your mind quickly. "No thanks."

But the woman has already popped open the can.

You hear a fizzing sound.

PSSSSSSSSSSSS.

A cloud of gas — misty white gas — escapes from the can!

The cloud grows so big, it fills the dining room. Thicker. Whiter. So thick, you choke. You can't see. . . .

"I can't breathe!" Jamie cries desperately.

Me, either! you think.

Take your last gasp on PAGE 53.

The ghost is at least seven feet tall. A huge, ugly, hulking, transparent form. Dressed in overalls. Like a janitor. Horrible tiny sunken eyes, like raisins, dot his huge puffy face.

At first, you can see right through him to the back of the elevator.

He looks half dead and half alive. You stare at him as his transparent body becomes solid.

In his right hand he carries a long, clattering chain. Each link of the chain is the size of a doughnut. He lifts it, gripping it in both hands as if he wants to strangle someone.

You!

Run as fast as you can to PAGE 105!

You and Jamie leap through the doors into the pitch-black elevator.

"Aaaahhhhh!" you scream as you fall.

"Aaaaaaahhhhhhhh!" Jamie's scream is even louder.

Both of you let out your cries of terror as you fall straight down . . .

Into a dark shaft . . .

Falling . . . falling . . .

Land on PAGE 72.

Jamie jumps up and starts pacing the room.

"Uh, there might only be six of them," he lies to the ghost. "Their names are Sleepy, Dopey, Doc, Grumpy, Happy, and Sneezy. Yeah. That's everybody. Just six of them."

"No!" the ghost shouts.

His voice booms in the room, shaking the lamps. The air turns so icy, you and Jamie both shiver as if you've stepped out into a snowy winter night.

"Don't lie to me!" the ghost yells. "I am as ancient as these walls, and I can sense the truth! There are seven of your dwarfs. You have two minutes to name the last one. Or die!"

Your heart starts racing almost as fast as your mind.

The seventh dwarf. Who is it?

"I know! It's Wimpy!" Jamie exclaims.

"No way," you moan. "Try again."

Jamie squeezes his eyes shut and thinks hard. "Uh, Lazy? Sneaky? Bashful? Stupid?"

You shrug. You just don't know. It can't be Lazy or Stupid, can it? Nah . . . but you've got to pick one!

If you think it's Bashful, turn to PAGE 59.
If you think it's Sneaky, turn to PAGE 41.

Sandy Brecker's eyes light up like neon dollar signs.

"I heard you singing," the ghost explains. "You kids have talent! You're great. Listen, I'm not supposed to leave this hotel. Ever. But for you I'm going to make an exception. I'm taking you to New York, to sign a record deal. Let's go."

Sandy leads you to a deserted area on the first floor, near some windows. It's a whole wall of glass, in fact.

He picks up a chair and throws it through the window.

"Why didn't we think of that?" Jamie pokes you in the side. "We could have gotten out of here *easy!*"

"Come on, kids," Sandy urges. "We've got to hurry."

Hurry? you think. Why hurry?

Then you hear an awful, moaning wind coming at your back — roaring through the hotel halls!

Do what Sandy said — and hurry to PAGE 76.

"Run?" you whisper. Jamie nods.

The two of you turn and race out of the room. You slam the door behind you and hurry down the hall to another hotel room. The stolen key unlocks it.

"At least we'll be safe in here," you declare as the two of you flop down on a bed. Then you spot a telephone. Your eyes light up. "Hey — we can call the police!"

Jamie shakes his head. "The police will never believe us," he argues. "What are we going to say? That the hotel is haunted?"

He reaches into his back pocket. "Maybe this will help." He whips out a glossy pamphlet. "I found this in the lobby," he explains. "Read it."

He tosses it to you, and you start to read.

"It's about the hotel," Jamie explains, not waiting for you to finish reading. "All about the Mortegarth family. They built this hotel. And it tells about this horrible stuff that happened years ago — in Room 402. I think Room 402 might be the key to finding Drew Mortegarth!"

Hmmm. Sounds interesting . . .

But wouldn't it be safer just to call the police?

If you want to call the police, turn to PAGE 31.

If you want to go to Room 402, turn to PAGE 42.

"Aaaahhhh!" Jamie screams as the truck roars toward you.

With a hard jerk, you yank the steering wheel to the right.

KA-BAM!

The bus bumps and jerks over the edge of the road, into a small ditch. Then it rolls on, crashing and smashing through a barbed-wire fence.

It finally stops. You've driven straight into the middle of a field of cows.

"Moooo!" the cows cry, startled by the bus's arrival.

"Ouch," you moan. You bounced against the steering wheel in the driver's seat. That hurt!

"Yay!" a crowd of voices behind you cheers.

Uh-oh.

Turn to PAGE 5.

"Helllp!" you scream. You struggle to escape from the ghost on the couch and the attacking newspaper.

"Go away!" a deep voice orders. It comes from somewhere near your knee. "We're old. Leave us alone!"

Then, across the room, you notice another newspaper fold itself up. It floats toward you.

An old, faded magazine rises up from an end table. Then a thick book. They sail in your direction.

Oh, no! The whole lobby is filled with invisible ghosts!

"Ow!" you cry as a hardcover book bonks you on the head.

The ghost holding your ankle shakes you harder. So hard that you topple sideways. You crash onto the couch beside him.

From above, a collection of newspapers and magazines swirls around. They hang over you, ready to strike.

"Noooo!" You cover your head with your arms.

But you can't stop them. The newspapers attack.

SMACK! WHACK! SMACK! They swat you on your back, your shoulders, your head.

"Ow! Ouch! Yeowww!" you wail.

Defend yourself, and turn to PAGE 39.

A small man dressed in knee-pants and a leather vest lopes toward you. A hat with a feather bobs on his curly hair. He has a small beard and shining blue eyes.

Just like the dwarfs in the movie!

Except for one thing. He doesn't look very friendly!

Without a word, he runs up to you and grabs you around the legs. Then he whips out a long rope — and ties you up!

"Hey!" Jamie shouts, coming to your rescue.

But two more dwarfs sneak up on Jamie from behind. They throw a large cloth bag over his head. Then four more dwarfs rush out of the woods to help. They tie Jamie's hands behind his back.

"Help!" Jamie cries. "Stop it! Let us go!"

But it's no use. The dwarfs drag you, kicking and screaming, into the woods — where they make you cook their food, clean their house all day, and even work in the mines!

And worst of all, they name *you* "Sneaky"!

Looks as if the old ghost was right. Dwarfs *are* dangerous!

THE END

"Give me a break!" you snap at Jamie. "I'm not going to eat that stupid mint. I don't want to die!"

Jamie rolls his eyes. "I *know* that, you jerk!" he mutters under his breath. "You were supposed to *pretend* to eat it. Then we could get out of here. But never mind. Let's run for it!"

Jamie takes off, running down the hall toward the elevator.

You follow him, your feet pounding the carpeted hallway.

You glance at the old-fashioned elevator dial ahead of you. It's a half-circle above the elevator door, with numbers for each floor. A brass hand sweeps around the numbers to indicate what floor the elevator is on.

"It's almost here! Keep running!" Jamie shouts.

Behind you, you can hear Moira's footsteps trotting after you. She doesn't run very fast. But you can feel the cold air moving closer. Closing in . . .

Just as you reach the elevator, the doors start to open.

"Keep running!" Jamie shouts.

No problem, you think. You couldn't stop if you wanted to.

And you definitely don't want to!

Leap into the elevator on PAGE 93.

"Lie down," Sara suggests. "Relax. I've got hot chocolate waiting for you."

She flips on a cassette player. Soft music begins to play. But it's not the kind of music you like.

You're listening to lullabies!

Automatically, you yawn. Jamie does too.

Sara dims the lights.

"Oh, no," Jamie groans, blinking to keep his eyes open. "It's a trap!"

"Sweet dreams," Sara says with an evil laugh.

Then she floats out of the room, passing right through the wall and out to the hallway.

Turn to PAGE 30.

You shudder and shiver violently, feeling the deep cold of the ghost as he passes through your body.

Then he floats out into the hall. In a moment, he is gone.

"Wow!" Jamie exclaims when the ghost has vanished. "Cool!"

"Yeah," you comment, yawning. "Now we know how to escape. If we can only stay awake. And survive."

Jamie eyes you. "So what should we do? Go back to the room?"

You shrug. "Maybe. Or maybe we should try to track down Drew Mortegarth. Or the others."

Jamie yawns. "I'm too tired to think," he confesses. "You decide."

So decide!

To hide out in your room until checkout time, turn to PAGE 73.

To keep searching the hotel, turn to PAGE 111.

Your teeth start chattering so hard, you can barely talk.

"Op-op-open that d-d-d-door," you chatter at Jamie.

You point to the small wooden door. The one on the far side of the freezer. The one Moira said would lead to Drew Mortegarth's secret room.

Jamie is shivering too. He rubs his arms with his hands to keep warm. It seems as if he doesn't want to stop rubbing them long enough to reach for the door.

But finally he edges close to it. He lifts the steel handle.

You and he peer into a small dark space on the other side of the wooden door.

"Wha-what's in there?" you stutter.

Find out on PAGE 114.

As soon as Jamie and Drew pass through the open doorway, you slam it shut.

BAM!

The ghosts are locked in forever.

Then you make a mad dash for Mrs. Matson's car.

She leaps into the driver's seat and starts the engine. You and the other kids pile into the back-seat.

"Yay!" you all cheer as she pulls out of the parking lot. "We made it! We escaped from the Dead Hotel!"

"And now, on to Washington!" Jamie announces with relief.

WHRRRRRRR ... WHIZ-WHRRRR ...

"Uh-oh," Mrs. Matson murmurs as she speeds down the deserted highway. "The engine still sounds bad. Maybe I should stop. . . ."

She glances out the window. So do you. You both spot an old, weird-looking house at the same time.

The sign in front says, WELCOME TO THE COZY COFFIN INN.

"No way!" B. J. shouts when he realizes what his mom is thinking. "Don't pull off there! Just keep going, Mom. Keep going until we see the White House!"

"All right," Mrs. Matson agrees with a nod.

And that's just what she does.

THE END

"Run!" you scream to the others.

You turn left and race down the hall. Your heart pounds as you push through an emergency door to a flight of stairs.

Stumbling, you take the steps two at a time. Down one flight. Then another. Another.

Your heart pounds harder and harder. You can hear footsteps behind you. And a clattering sound.

The sound of the chain dragging on the stairs! *CLANG! CLATTER-CLANG-CLANG!*

Your terror grows as the sound comes closer.

Finally, as you round the corner on the last flight of stairs, you dare to glance back.

There's a person standing right above you.

You stop dead in your tracks.

Find out who it is on PAGE 110.

You shiver as the cold air moves closer.

Closer.

"Noooo!" you scream in terror. The sheer terror of knowing that there are ghosts in the room.

You can't see them. You don't know how many.

But you can feel their coldness. The horrible chill up and down your neck. Your whole spine.

If only I hadn't dialed 911, you think.

What a mistake! You picked up the phone — and led the ghosts right to you. They traced the call!

Your heart pounds as you inch off the bed. Toward the door.

"Don't try to escape!" a man's voice warns. He chuckles. "You haven't even tried out the hotel swimming pool yet!"

Swimming pool? Uh-oh.

Do you know how to swim?

If you know how to swim, turn to PAGE 74.

If you don't know how to swim, turn to PAGE 119.

You pop open a bottle of clam juice and take a swig.

"It doesn't taste so bad," you tell Jamie.

Maybe not. But it *is* magic — like everything else in this haunted hotel.

Come on — doesn't drinking clam juice sound just a little bit . . . fishy?

Too late now. You'll just have to find out for yourself what drinking the clam juice does to you. You see, it affects everyone differently.

Some unlucky kids discovered it made let ers disa pear from th page of t e book they were readi g. . . .

So here's some advice. N xt time you v sit the hot l, don t eat *an thing*! We wou dn t want *you* to dis pear in . . .

THE E D.

You can't fight the magic of the room. You sink into the pillows and begin to drift off. You're half awake . . . half asleep . . . half dreaming. . . .

You half dream about the Seven Dwarfs. Except that you dream their names are Burpy, Sloppy, Messy, Grouchy, Snoozy, Sleazy, and Drew Mortegarth.

Something snaps you out of the dream. Were you thinking about Drew Mortegarth? And the chance to escape?

"Whoa!" you cry, your eyes snapping open.

You gulp air. Did you almost fall asleep?

Yes. Almost.

You sit up and shake your head.

And gasp.

A ghost is materializing in front of you.

It takes a moment for him to come into view. But when you see his solid form, you want to scream.

Turn to PAGE 121.

You grip the door handle tightly.

Don't scream. Don't run away, you tell yourself.

Just hold the door open for Jamie and Drew!

Shrieking, the pack of ghosts rushes toward you.

It only takes one quick glance to tell you who they are.

The Mortegarth ghosts! The hideous ones from the broom closet.

They wave their arms wildly as they race for the door.

"Jamie! Drew! Hurry up!" you urge.

The ghosts are in front of Jamie. They reach the front door first. . . .

But the minute they lurch for the opening, they stop. As if the fresh air — and the outside world — were some kind of brick wall. Halting them. Turning them back.

They stumble away from the open door, moaning.

And Jamie and Drew rush through!

Hold the door open until you turn to PAGE 104.

"Jamie?" you gasp.

Jamie stands above you, dragging the ghost's metal chain. "I grabbed this away from the ghost!" Jamie explains, holding up the chain. "He wasn't as strong as he looked."

You shake your head, amazed. "What about Moira and B. J.?"

Jamie shrugs. "They ran the other way. Come on — let's go find that Drew Mortegarth."

He drops the chain, and you both hurry down the last flight of stairs. You step into a large, carpeted hallway.

It's empty and eerily quiet. Until you hear a low growl behind you. You whirl around.

A large black dog appears out of thin air. A ghost dog!

The dog barks at you viciously. Then he dashes past you down the hall — toward an exit door.

"Look," you cry. "A way out."

You race after the dog. He pushes through a rubber flap in the bottom section of the door. A built-in doggie door.

You try the knob. Locked. "How about that?" you suggest, pointing to the doggie door.

Jamie squints at you. "Are you serious?"

Are you? Can you squeeze through a doggie door?

If you try to follow the dog, turn to PAGE 37.

If you keep looking for Drew Mortegarth, turn to PAGE 17.

"Let's keep moving," you decide. "Otherwise I'll fall asleep for sure."

Jamie yawns and nods. "Deal."

You and Jamie sneak through the hallways. Using the stolen desk clerk key, you peek into the empty rooms.

No Drew Mortegarth. No Moira or B. J.

"I'm sick of this," Jamie complains. By now you've made it to the fourth floor. You unlock Room 402.

"Do you have a better idea?" you demand as you push open the door.

Then you gasp!

Find out what's in Room 402 on PAGE 132.

Your invisible opponent keeps shaking your ankles. You spin your arms like windmills to keep from losing your balance.

"Helllp!" you scream.

Any second, you're going to topple over backwards and crack your skull on the marble floor!

You take a swing at the ghost. But it's really hard to aim at someone invisible. Your hand hits something yucky.

What is that? A face? A mouth? Wet, toothless gums?

Eww!

You swing again and feel hair. Yeah. Hair on its head.

You yank hard.

"Ow!" the ghost cries.

You hear a rustling sound again. Out of the corner of your eye you see something moving. You glance over.

Uh-oh. There's a newspaper floating in midair!

It seems to be rolling itself up, the same way your dad rolls up a newspaper to swat a fly.

Like a weapon.

The newspaper rushes toward you. It swings back and lets loose with a hard swat to your head!

Turn to PAGE 98.

"Follow me," you call to Moira, B. J., and B. J.'s mom. "We've got to take the stairs — no matter what the ghosts do!"

Your heart pounds as you push your way up the steps. Past the crowd of ghosts.

"Staaaaay," the ghosts moan.

Freezing cold hands touch your face. Your hair. Your shoulders and back.

"Nooooo," the ghosts cry. "Don't go."

They grab at your arms and tug on your clothes. But you push on. You keep climbing. Your teeth chatter from the cold. Your skin crawls as each ghost pulls at you, begging you to stay.

"Leave me alone!" Moira screams. "Let go!"

Behind you, you can hear Mrs. Matson whimpering. Even she is scared to death!

At the top of the stairs, you open a door. You race for the broom closet near the lobby, where Jamie and Drew Mortegarth are waiting for you.

"What time is it?" you call desperately to B. J.

"It's eleven o' clock!" he hollers back. "Time's up!"

Don't even check your watch. Just hurry to PAGE 83!

114

Your eyes finally adjust to the dark. A tiny bit of light from the meat locker filters into the adjoining room.

Then you see what's behind the wooden door.

Nothing.

"It's not Drew Mortegarth's secret room. It's just another part of the f-f-freezer!" Jamie wails. "Moira t-t-tricked us!"

You try to answer him, but you're shivering too hard.

You suddenly remember the last thing you said to Moira. "Where's the meat?"

Now you know.

You're the meat.

Dead meat!

THE END

"Yaaaiii!" Jamie screams as you speed down the dark road toward the oncoming truck.

BEEEP! BEEEE-EEEP!

The approaching truck is a huge semitrailer. One of those mammoth things with eighteen wheels. The driver honks his horn at you. Over and over.

BEEEEEPPP!

You can see him waving his arm, trying to get you to move over. You're right in his lane!

"I'm trying!" you shout as you pull on the wheel.

With all your strength, you try to turn the bus's steering wheel to the right.

But the wheel won't turn. It's stuck!

And no matter how hard you try to stomp on the brakes with your feet, the bus keeps picking up speed.

Faster. Faster.

BEEEEEEEEEEEP!

You close your eyes. You can't stand to watch. . . .

"Oh, no!" Jamie screams in terror.

Open your eyes on PAGE 118.

116

The spikes on the desk clerk's head zoom toward you.

"Run!" you shout. You duck around Horner Smithfield and race down the hall.

You don't look back. But you hear Jamie following.

You jam the brass key into one of the room doors.

Bingo! It opens. You and Jamie dash in, slam the door shut, and lock it. Luckily the room is empty. No guests — no ghosts.

At least none that you can see.

"Whoa," Jamie exclaims, flopping down on one of two double beds. "Talk about a bad-hair day!"

"Who's having a bad-hair day?" a girl calls out.

You stiffen. Where did that voice come from? The closet?

You and Jamie eye each other. Now what? you wonder, gulping.

"Let's get out of here," Jamie whispers.

You're not so sure. That voice sounds familiar. Should you open the closet to see who it is?

If you open the closet door, turn to PAGE 10.

If you slip quietly out of the room, turn to PAGE 96.

You'd like to stay in the hotel. You'd like to help Moira, B. J., and Mrs. Matson.

But Jamie's right. It's better to get out now. While you still have the chance.

"Okay," you tell Jamie. "We'll do it your way."

You dart out the door and into the cold, dark night.

BAM!

The door slams behind you.

"Where to?" Jamie asks, staring at the empty road.

You gaze into the woods behind the hotel. A rustling sound comes from the bushes.

"Let's head toward the road," you answer. Those woods are way too dark and creepy to investigate.

You take a few steps, shivering. It's chilly outside.

Then something small darts across your path. You stare and rub your eyes.

"I can't believe it," you murmur to Jamie. "It's a dwarf!"

Turn to PAGE 99.

118

Good thing you closed your eyes.

It wasn't pretty.

You drove straight into the truck.

KA-SMASH!

But it wasn't because you're a bad driver. You don't have lousy hand-eye coordination or anything. . . .

It's because the invisible ghost bus driver was sitting on the floor near your feet — and pushing on the gas pedal!

With his other hand, he was holding the steering wheel so you couldn't turn it.

Pretty sneaky, those ghosts. What will they think of next?

Correction: What will *you* think of next? How about the way this adventure has come to an

END?

Six strong hands lift you up. Six *invisible* hands.

Two of them grab one arm. Two grab the other. And two grab your legs.

"Hellllp! Let me go!" you scream.

Near the door, you see Jamie suddenly rise into the air.

At least that's how it looks. But you know ghosts must be lifting him too.

"Heelllllp!" Jamie screams, kicking at the air.

No matter how hard you struggle, you can't get loose from the ghosts.

You kick and swing your fists. But you can't see what you're swinging at.

Before you know it, the ghosts have carried you down the stairs and out a back door.

To the hotel's swimming pool.

A crescent moon hovers over the trees that surround the pool. Owls hoot in the distance.

But you barely notice.

All you can see is the swimming pool.

And the fact that there's no water in it!

Turn to PAGE 123.

Your eyes widen when you see what's inside.

A head!

A woman's head. Resting on the pile of tiny ice cubes.

"Aaaaaaaahhh!" You and Jamie shriek together.

It's B. J.'s mom!

Mrs. Matson reaches a chilly hand up from the ice bin. She slides the door open all the way.

"Mrs. Matson?" Jamie gasps. His voice is choked with terror.

"The ghosts got me," Mrs. Matson explains, climbing out of the ice bin. Her eyes narrow as she takes a step toward you. "And now I'm going to get you!"

And that's just what she does.

Oh, well. Don't feel too bad. What did you expect? You were doomed the moment you checked into this haunted hotel.

You never had a ghost of a chance!

THE END

The ghost is hideous. He has oozing, rotting skin. His teeth are yellow and pitted. His shoulder-length hair is filthy.

And he stinks! His clothes smell as if they haven't been washed in a hundred years.

"Sweet dreams," he greets you. "We almost had you. Lie down, now. Go back to sleep and have sweet dreams. . . ."

"No!" you shout, fighting to stay awake. You grab Jamie and shake him. He sits bolt upright.

"What's going on?" he mumbles. "Did we name all the dwarfs?"

"Dwarfs?" The ghost repeats the word fearfully. He backs away. "What dwarfs?"

"The Seven Dwarfs," Jamie replies. "We were trying to remember their names."

The ghost wrinkles his forehead. "I don't like dwarfs," he complains. "They're dangerous. Listen, I'll make you a deal. Tell me their names so I can watch out for them. And I'll let you live."

You and Jamie exchange glances.

Uh-oh. Can you name them all?

Cross your fingers, and turn to PAGE 94.

Jamie frowns, looking worried.

"Yeah," he mutters. "Drew is right. Our watches *could* be wrong."

You gulp, imagining it. Racing for the front door. The ghosts chasing you. And then — you can't get out, because it's locked. Just because your watch was off by one minute!

That would be horrible. Too horrible.

But suddenly you have an idea. "Hey!" you exclaim. "We know someone whose watch is *always* right. Don't we, Jamie?"

Jamie grins and nods. "B. J.!" he cheers.

B. J. is a wimp and a nerd. But he's a total time fanatic. You know his watch will be right. He checks it twenty times a day against the clocks at school.

"I'll go find B. J.," you declare, opening the closet door.

"Just be careful," Drew cautions you. "And be back here by eleven o'clock!"

Turn to PAGE 7.

Face it. You could have ten Olympic swimming medals, and it wouldn't help you now.

The ghosts carry you and Jamie to the high diving board. Holding you in midair, they start to bounce.

"And-a-one . . . and-a-two . . ."

On the count of three, the ghosts toss you into the pool.

No fair, you think as you hit the bottom of the empty pool. Then you remember something your uncle used to say. That you were going to make a big splash in life.

Oh, well.

You'll have to settle for a big *SPLAT* instead!

THE END

There *is* no door!

The wall behind the skeletons is solid brick!

There's no way out.

But you've got another problem. An even worse one.

You've moved the bones to a bad spot. You've blocked your only exit — up the stairs!

Oh, well. You can move them back later, you think. You're *soooo* tired!

Yawning, you lie down to take a nap. A *long* nap.

When you wake up again, you are a ghost — with your own bones added to the enormous pile!

No bones about it — this is

THE END.

You close your eyes tight and slam on the brakes.

EEEEE! The brakes make a horrible squealing noise as the bus screeches to a halt.

Then — silence. You listen, your eyes still closed.

Finally, you open your eyes. "What happened?" you whisper.

You gaze into the dark night. The road ahead is empty.

"Didn't you see?" Jamie cries. "I thought we were road pizza! And then ... it passed right through us!"

"*What* passed right through us?" you demand.

"The truck!" Jamie replies. "It was a ghost truck! It came straight at us. Then — zoom! It drove right through us!"

A big smile spreads across your lips.

We made it! you think. We survived the haunted hotel!

You start to whoop and give Jamie a high five. But then you freeze. You just thought of something awful.

"Wait a minute," you mutter. "Hold it right there."

You hop out of the truck and dash toward the field of cows.

Turn to PAGE 29.

"Hold it!" You squint suspiciously at Moira. "How can you still be cold *now*? I mean, you've been hiding in the closet. The cold air from the freezer wouldn't cling to you *that* long."

Moira gives you a nasty glare. "We were in there a *long* time," she snaps. "If you don't believe me, just ask B. J.'s mom. She was with us."

B. J.'s mom? Your eyes widen. You wonder if she's become a ghost too.

"Where is she now?" Jamie asks.

"In the secret room," Moira answers. "With Drew Mortegarth."

"Okay," Jamie agrees. "Take us there."

He starts to follow her down the hall. But you're still not sure. You reach out and grab Moira's arm.

It's cold. Ice-cold.

She *must* be a ghost! you think.

But what if she's not? What if she's telling the truth? What if she can lead you to B. J.'s mom — and Drew Mortegarth?

If you're still sure Moira is a ghost, turn to PAGE 90.

If you're not sure, and you want to believe her story, turn to PAGE 84.

"Hey! What about Drew?" Jamie protests as Mrs. Matson speeds down the deserted highway. "We've got to go back for him!"

You nod and start to agree. But you're so tired. So sleepy . . .

You lean back in the corner of your seat and close your eyes. Drew's words echo in your head as you doze off.

"Sweet dreams . . ."

Hours later, you wake up and glance around. Out the car window, you can see the Capitol building.

You made it to Washington, D.C.!

"We're here!" B. J.'s mom chirps.

You blink. "Wow," you mutter. "What happened? What about the car trouble? And how did you guys escape from the Hotel Morte?"

Mrs. Matson twists her head around to glance at you in the backseat. "What car trouble?" she asks. "What Hotel Morte? We've been driving for eight hours straight. And you've been sleeping the whole way!"

Was it really all just a dream?

Sorry. There are some things you'll never know in

THE END.

128

You leap into the bus driver's seat. It's empty.

"He's gone!" you shout, gripping the huge steering wheel.

The wheel is so big, you can hardly control it. And the seat is high. Your feet don't quite reach the pedals. You have to slump down and stretch your legs way out.

Your heart lunges into your throat. You can hardly breathe.

"Whoa!" Jamie shouts. "Look out!"

Up ahead, there's a huge truck. Coming straight at you!

You grip the wheel for dear life and stare into the dark night.

To your left is a sheer, rocky cliff. You can't go that way.

To your right is a fenced-in field. Filled with cows.

Straight ahead is the truck!

Quick — decide what to do!

If you try to go straight, turn to PAGE 115.

If you swerve into the field of cows, turn to PAGE 97.

If you slam on the brakes, close your eyes, and hope for the best, turn to PAGE 125.

What *am* I waiting for? you wonder.

Then you realize.

"Moira," you answer. "And B. J. and his mom. We can't just leave them here — can we?"

"We have to," Jamie argues. "We'll go get help. If we don't leave now, we might all be stuck here forever."

You stare at the road. There's not a car in sight.

"Maybe we should stay and find them," you argue. "And then lead them out through this door."

"No one can open this door except me," the old ghost informs you. "Go now — or lose the chance forever!"

"Come on!" Jamie urges. "Let's go!"

You want to leave. But should you? Finding Drew Mortegarth might be the only way for *everyone* to escape the hotel alive.

Well?

If you walk through the secret door, turn to PAGE 117.

If you stay and look for Drew Mortegarth, turn to PAGE 79.

You and Jamie leave Room 402 and head for the dining room.

Drew Mortegarth said he was waiting for you there.

Of course, maybe "he" is really a "she." You couldn't tell from the whispering voice on the phone.

You hurry to the huge dining room on the main floor. It's filled with tables, each one set for dinner. White tablecloths drape to the floor.

Seated at a table right in the middle of the room — under the chandelier — is a beautiful young woman. She's wearing a red silk dress and a diamond necklace. Her blond hair is piled high on her head.

"Hello," she says softly. She has a deep voice and a warm smile. "I'm Drew Mortegarth. I've been waiting for you."

Turn to PAGE 19.

You decide to take Moira's word and follow the skeleton's advice.

Why not? You don't have any better ideas about how to escape this haunted hotel.

You and Moira lift the bones and skulls one at a time. Moving them from one side of the basement to the other.

It's like playing pick-up sticks. You have to be *sooooo* careful. You get so involved in moving the bones that you don't notice the truth.

But after four hours, you finally glance up and see.

See what you see on PAGE 124.

132

There, in the middle of the room, is a dark stain of blood. It forms a circle about two feet wide.

As you stare at it, the blood spreads into a wider and wider pool.

It's as if the floor itself is bleeding!

Don't scream. Just turn to PAGE 46.

The wrong book?

"What do you mean, we're in the wrong book?" you ask.

The red-and-purple-haired girl shrugs. "Simple. If you've got a genie popping out of a cola can, you *should* be in the GIVE YOURSELF GOOSE-BUMPS book called *Scream of the Evil Genie!*"

"Hey, that sounds cool!" Jamie cries. "I wish we *were* in that book — instead of this one!"

"No problem," the genie replies. "But just remember: When you get there, you've already used up one wish!"

With that, the world goes dark. And spins.

And when you open your eyes again, you're in a completely different story.

Luckily for you, it's a story that is nowhere near

THE END!

"Thanks for showing us the secret door," you tell the ghost. "But we really can't leave without the others."

The smelly old ghost shrugs. "Suit yourself." He slams the door closed. "You'll regret it."

Then he floats up toward the ceiling and vanishes.

"Whoa," Jamie murmurs.

"Let's get back to our room," you urge. "This place is creeping me out."

You and Jamie sneak back to your floor. As you head toward your room, you notice a flash of movement out of the corner of your eye.

The ice machine. It's sliding open.

By itself.

Quick! Go on to PAGE 120!

"Whoa!" you cry, jerking back.

The man twists a knob on the TV, turning up the sound. In the next instant, he yanks his airy arm back. Back into the TV picture. Then he returns to solid form.

He laughs a horrible, evil laugh.

You and Jamie tremble. Moira gasps.

"Yikes!" B. J. cries. He drops the remote control. "The guy's a ghost!"

The man sneers, still chuckling. "You have just checked into a haunted hotel," he explains. "And not just for one night — but forever! By morning, you will all be ghosts. We hope you'll enjoy your stay. It will last until *eternity*!"

Turn to PAGE 49.

About R.L. Stine

R.L. Stine is the most popular author in America. He is the creator of the *Goosebumps, Give Yourself Goosebumps, Fear Street,* and *Ghosts of Fear Street* series, among other popular books. He has written more than 100 scary novels for kids. Bob lives in New York City with his wife, Jane, teenage son, Matt, and dog, Nadine.

SOLUTION TO
GIVE YOURSELF GOOSEBUMPS
SPECIAL EDITION #1
THE ULTIMATE CHALLENGE:
INTO THE JAWS OF DOOM

Here are the section numbers that you must read, *in this order*, to defeat the Super Computer and make it out of the Hall of Incredible Science. Note: This is the *shortest* possible path. There are a few detours you can make along the way, but you cannot escape without going to these locations in this order.

Fourth Floor: 1-89-101-19-97-131-180-220-166-60 (Space Travel Room)-148-117-35-160 (get Fire Extinguisher)-41-166-207 (Aerodynamics Room)-213-171 (get Boomerang)-108-151-58-203-178-159-166-60 (Space Travel Room again)-223-183 (get Space Glove)-231-133-130-69-209-229-64-93-47

Fire Stairs: 156-28-206

Third Floor: 54-205-194-216 (Wonder of Life Room)-83-49-127-17-162-63 (get Key)-194-141-134 (get Compass)-113-196 (get Walkie-talkie)-98-88 (get Stink Bomb)-193 (Waves and Motion Room)-138 (Maze)-95-154-173-236-111 (get Laser)-202-224-40-4-194-190

140

Fire Stairs: 51-80-120-237-27-175

First Floor: 126

Second Floor: 212-23-161-227 (Electricity Room)-132-225-189-165-118-11-74 (get Electric Motor)-13-197-99-187 (Thinking Machines Room)-147-85-112-155-48-76-105 (get P.D.A.)-45-103-94-221 (get Crash Code)-179-232-16-124-143-57-201-163-70-168-107-78-238.

GET READY.

The aliens have landed.
Their mission: To squeeze you dry.

GOOSEBUMPS ®
SERIES 2000
R.L. STINE

The Continuing Story...

Book #5: Invasion of the Body Squeezers: Part II

The next millenium will shock you.

In bookstores this May.

SCHOLASTIC

 PARACHUTE

❏ BAB56887-6	#50	Calling All Creeps!	
❏ BAB56888-4	#51	Beware, the Snowman	
❏ BAB56889-2	#52	How I Learned to Fly	
❏ BAB56890-6	#53	Chicken Chicken	
❏ BAB56891-4	#54	Don't Go to Sleep!	
❏ BAB56892-2	#55	The Blob That Ate Everyone	
❏ BAB56893-0	#56	The Curse of Camp Cold Lake	
❏ BAB56894-9	#57	My Best Friend Is Invisible	
❏ BAB56895-7	#58	Deep Trouble II	
❏ BAB56897-3	#59	The Haunted School	
❏ BAB39053-8	#60	Werewolf Skin	
❏ BAB39986-1	#61	I Live in Your Basement!	
❏ BAB39987-X	#62	Monster Blood IV	
❏ BAB35007-2		Goosebumps Triple Header #1	$4.50
❏ BAB62836-4		Tales to Give You Goosebumps Special Edition #1: Book & Light Set	$11.95
❏ BAB48993-3		Tales to Give You Goosebumps Special Edition #1	$3.99
❏ BAB26603-9		More Tales to Give You Goosebumps Special Edition #2: Book & Light Set	$11.95
❏ BAB26002-0		More Tales to Give You Goosebumps Special Edition #2	$3.99
❏ BAB74150-4		Even More Tales to Give You Goosebumps Special Edition #3: Book and Boxer Shorts Pack	$14.99
❏ BAB73909-3		Even More Tales to Give You Goosebumps Special Edition #3	$3.99
❏ BAB88132-9		Still More Tales to Give You Goosebumps Special Edition #4: Scare Pack	$11.95
❏ BAB23795-0		More & More Tales to Give You Goosebumps Special Edition #5: Book and Cap Pack	$11.95
❏ BAB34119-7		Goosebumps Fright Light Edition	$12.95
❏ BAB36682-3		More & More & More Tales to Give You Goosebumps Special Edition #6: Book and Holiday Stocking Set	$9.95
❏ BAB53770-9		The Goosebumps Monster Blood Pack	$11.95
❏ BAB50995-0		The Goosebumps Monster Edition #1	$12.95
❏ BAB93371-X		The Goosebumps Monster Edition #2	$12.95
❏ BAB36673-4		The Goosebumps Monster Edition #3	$12.95
❏ BAB60265-9		The Goosebumps Official Collector's Caps Collecting Kit	$5.99
❏ BAB73906-9		The Goosebumps Postcard Book	$7.95
❏ BAB31259-6		The Goosebumps Postcard Book II	$7.95
❏ BAB32717-8		The 1998 Goosebumps 365 Scare-a-Day Calendar	$8.95
❏ BAB10485-3		The Goosebumps 1998 Wall Calendar	$10.99

• •

Scare me, thrill me, mail me GOOSEBUMPS now!

Available wherever you buy books, or use this order form.
Scholastic Inc., P.O. Box 7502, Jefferson City, MO 65102

Please send me the books I have checked above. I am enclosing $_____ (please add $2.00 to cover shipping and handling). Send check or money order—no cash or C.O.D.s please.

Name _____Age _____

Address_____

City _____State/Zip_____

Please allow four to six weeks for delivery. Offer good in the U.S. only. Sorry, mail orders are not available to residents of Canada. Prices subject to change.

Log on for Scares!
Scholastic presents
G
TM
Goosebumps®
ON THE WEB!
ttp://www.scholastic.com/goosebumps
The latest books!
Start your own Goosebumps reading club!
Author R.L. Stine's tips on writing!
Really gross recipes!
Craft ideas!
How to get Goosebumps stuff: sportswear, CD-ROMs, video releases and more!
Exclusive contests!
Interactive word games and activities!
1997 Parachute Press, Inc. GOOSEBUMPS is a registered trademark of Parachute Press, Inc. All rights reserved.
GWEB1296